STUMPED

MAPLE SYRUP MYSTERIES 13

EMILY JAMES

Editor: Christopher Saylor at www.saylorediting.wordpress.com/services/

Cover Design: Deranged Doctor Design at www.derangeddoctordesign.com

Published February 2020 by Stronghold Books

Ebook ISBN: 978-1-988480-41-1; Print Book ISBN: 978-1-988480-42-8; Large Print ISBN: 978-1-988480-56-5

FREE BOOK OFFER

Sign up for the author's mailing list and get a free copy of *Sapped*, the prequel to *A Sticky Inheritance*. Visit www.smarturl.it/emilyjames to get started.

ALSO BY EMILY JAMES

Maple Syrup Mysteries

Sapped: A Maple Syrup Mysteries Prequel

A Sticky Inheritance

Bushwhacked

Almost Sleighed

Murder on Tap

Deadly Arms

Capital Obsession

Tapped Out

Bucket List

End of the Line

Slay Bells Ringing

(also contains a Cupcake Truck Mystery novella)

Rooted in Murder

Guilty or Knot

Stumped

Cupcake Truck Mysteries

Sugar and Vice

A Sampling of Murder (Coming Soon!)

To all of you who asked me for more Maple Syrup Mysteries. Thank you for loving these stories and these characters as much as I do.

The truth is more important than the facts.

— Frank Lloyd Wright

The one thing keeping me from wanting to mail Anderson all the paperwork I'd been buried under since he left on vacation was the knowledge that he'd have to run our law firm without me while I was on maternity leave. I hadn't spent this much time in my office at our firm the whole time we'd been working together.

I flipped to the next sheet of paper and tried to remind myself that Anderson hadn't had a vacation in five years, since long before I'd met him. He might not have even taken this one, except he planned to propose to his girlfriend while they were in the Bahamas. He'd dragged me along to every jewelry shop within a two-hour radius to help him pick out the ring. He could face down hostile witnesses, sweet-talk a jury, and out-debate the savviest prosecuting attorneys in Michigan, but the idea of having to pick out the perfect engagement ring had him so nervous he couldn't breathe without loosening his tie.

I'd tried not to tease him. Much. It was so out of character that I couldn't help ribbing him a little.

Though he was getting his revenge now, even if he didn't know it. I'd much rather be doing almost anything at Sugarwood than sitting here, double-checking work that our new junior lawyer should have felt confident to take care of himself.

Unfortunately, Sugarwood business wasn't going to save me this time. Not only was it the offseason for maple syrup production, but Russ had taken to hovering around me worse than a mother hen when a fox was eyeing up her chicks. You'd think it was his baby rather than Mark's and mine I was carrying.

The dizzy spells I'd been having this week only made things worse. I had the misfortune of experiencing the first one when Russ, Stacey, and I were discussing whether to upgrade any equipment this year. I'd been lucky to escape that meeting without Russ calling an ambulance. He'd wanted me to stay in bed until I could see a doctor. The compromise had been that I wouldn't drive myself anywhere.

I stretched out my lower back and slid the briefs back across my desk to Jay. "All's good."

He smiled at me a little too big, showing off his gums along with his teeth. He always reminded me a bit of a chipmunk, though I couldn't pin down why. "There's just one more thing. I'll run to my office and get it. It's for the appeal Mr. Taylor wanted me to file while he's gone."

He leaped up and was out of my office before I could stop him. And I'd thought I was nervous about making a mistake when I was fresh out of law school. Jay put me to shame in that department.

The phone on my desk buzzed in the way that let me know our receptionist was trying to reach me. If I was really lucky, Mark had arrived early to drive me home and the appeal paperwork would have to wait until I came back in on Friday. My eyes were starting to cross and blur.

I picked up the receiver. "Please say my ride's here."

"Ms. Fitzhenry-Dawes." Laini's voice had a tiny quiver to it underneath her forced professional tone.

The fact that she'd used my last name rather than calling me Nicole told me we likely had a client in reception. The shake in her voice though…I couldn't think of a good reason for that.

"Is everything alright?"

"There's a potential client here asking for you."

Laini knew I didn't take on a client unless they were innocent. That could potentially explain the strange note to her voice, but she shouldn't have sounded almost afraid. This wouldn't be the first time I'd spoken to a potential new client who would later be represented by Anderson. It wouldn't even be the first time a potential client had shown up without an appointment.

Maybe she was simply concerned about overstressing me, given the dizzy spells and how close I was to my due date. If I collapsed, Laini would have to explain to Anderson why she hadn't run better interference.

But speaking to a potential client would be more fun than reading over an appeal that—based on what I'd seen of Jay's work—didn't need me to check it.

"Send them back."

She breathed in and then out. "I'll tell them you'll be up as soon as you can."

Something tickled at the bottom of my throat where my collarbones met. She'd heard me. Then she'd hesitated.

For some reason, Laini didn't want me to be alone back here with whoever was out there. And she'd sounded afraid.

We'd never had an angry family member of a victim or an angry family member of a client we failed to acquit come to the office. My parents had never even had that happen. They had received threats. Someone might conceivably take it to the next step. Our world seemed to be going that way. People walked into Walmart with a gun and started shooting, after all.

Laini wouldn't have called me up if someone was there with a gun, though. At least, I didn't think she would. People would often do surprising things when their own life was in jeopardy.

Jay appeared in my doorway, a sheaf of papers in his hands. I held a finger to my lips and waved him in. He sat in the chair he'd vacated only minutes before like an obedient puppy.

What was I going to tell him? If I said *stay here in case there's a crazy man or woman with a gun up there,* and then it turned out to be nothing, he'd think I was crazy myself the rest of the time he worked for us. While I didn't want to be stuck checking his work for the next ten years, I did want him to respect me as a senior partner in the firm.

So maybe I'd give him half a truth. "I have a potential new client waiting up front. I'd like you to stay here. We don't want to give the impression that we're not busy by having us both go to greet him."

Jay gave a smile-eye roll. "Non-lawyers never understand how much goes into even a single sheet of paper."

The way he said it made me think he might be a lawyer's child as well as a lawyer himself, the way I was. If his lawyer parent helped him get the job here, it'd also explain why he seemed extra eager to please.

Focus, Nik. You have more important puzzles to solve.

I must be more nervous about what would greet me up front

than I wanted to admit. My brain was doing its run-in-circles-to-avoid-the-problem thing.

I was probably blowing this up well beyond the truth anyway. My paranoia seemed to have grown in size in time with my belly. After my last case, where I'd almost been run down by a truck while already pregnant, I'd had to face how I was basically my baby's shield against the world. He or she depended on me to keep them alive. It made everything seem so much more dangerous.

I stepped out the door of my office as if nothing were the matter. As soon as I knew Jay couldn't see me, I flattened against the wall. Sort of. My belly and my chest both stuck out. But it was enough to keep me hidden from anyone in the reception area unless they walked right in front of the doorway leading into the hallway. Our office and the one next door had once been part of a single large building. When whoever turned them into separate spaces dropped a wall down the middle, they'd done it in such a way that it left our hallway door off-center. As long as I scuttled sideways, I'd be out of sight until I could get a look at what was going on.

I'd look silly, but I wouldn't be taking chances while carrying my baby around. Assuming whoever was up front didn't have a gun or a knife, this would be a funny story to tell Mark when he came to pick me up.

He'd even be proud that I'd been so careful.

I shuffled along the wall until I reached the doorway. It'd be easier to peek out of without being spotted if it'd actually had a door on it, but it didn't, so I'd have to make do.

I strained my ears. Footsteps. Someone paced back and forth along the floor. The steps sounded too heavy to be a woman's. Other than that, the only other sound was the ticking of the cute scales-of-justice clock Laini kept on her desk.

I waited for the footsteps to head away from the doorway so the man would be facing away from me.

I poked my head around the doorframe.

The man's hands were empty of weapons.

And caked with what looked like dried blood.

2

What kind of a person drove to a lawyer's office with blood still on their hands? said a slightly frenetic voice in my head.

The kind who needs a lawyer, my mom's calmer voice reminded me.

Right. If he had that much blood on his hands, he likely had blood on him elsewhere, which explained Laini's freaked-out undertone and why she hadn't wanted to send him back to my office, where we'd be alone.

But if he'd come here, he also wasn't likely to hurt us. Whatever he'd done to end up covered in blood, he'd come here for help.

Anderson couldn't have predicted something like this would turn up while he was away, but he was going to owe me a big slice of chocolate cake when he got back. In the meantime, I'd have to deal with this until Anderson returned. This kind of client would definitely not be one for me to defend.

I drew in a deep breath and exhaled a prayer just in case the man had come here to kill us all, then pasted on the confident expression

I hoped mirrored my mom's. She could have been standing in the reception area when a blood-covered man came in and she wouldn't have even given an extra blink.

I might not be as unflappable as my parents, but they'd taught me well. Whatever came next, I needed to be in control of this situation and sound more confident than I felt.

I stepped into the reception area. "Sorry it took me so long. I had to wrap up what I was working on."

The man turned toward me, and Laini slumped in her chair ever so slightly, as if she'd barely been holding herself together.

The blood wasn't confined to the man's hands. He wore green-and-black plaid pajama pants and a Detroit Red Wings t-shirt that had once been white with the red, winged wheel on the front. The sports logo wasn't the only red on his shirt anymore.

It was a lot of blood. Enough that whoever it belonged to probably wasn't alive anymore. It certainly didn't belong to him, or he'd be showing signs of pain or dizziness.

"I'm Nicole Fizhenry-Dawes." I nodded toward his hands. "It looks like we'd better not shake."

His gaze locked on my face, and his shoulders lowered slightly, as if he were even more relieved than Laini to see me.

He held his hands up, and his gaze shifted to them. He stared at them for a long time. Long enough that Laini shifted behind her desk like she was considering whether or not to call the police.

"I don't know what happened," he finally said.

Was he in shock? His skin had a funny blue-gray cast to it, and a sheen of sweat covered his forehead.

Shock probably meant that it wasn't premeditated, whoever he'd killed. Unfortunately, this also didn't look like self-defense. People who killed someone in self-defense generally called the police rather than getting in their car with the blood still on them and driving to a lawyer's office.

For a second, the thought felt callous, but I'd been trained to think that way. When most parents were doing multiplication flash cards with their kids, my parents were drilling me on the different types of murder, grooming me to follow in their footsteps.

"Why don't you sit?" I gestured to the chairs behind him, then put my hand on my belly. Couldn't hurt to draw attention to the fact that I was a pregnant woman, just in case he was dangerous. Very few people are willing to hurt a pregnant woman. "It'll be better for both of us, okay?"

He nodded and did as I instructed. Unless he'd had a psychotic break that led to him killing someone, he didn't strike me as a threat.

"I don't know…" He moved his hands up and down in front of him over where the bloodstain was still drying on his shirt. "I woke up this way."

Crap. He was either lying or a psychotic break wasn't entirely out of the question.

Something tight wormed around in my chest. It felt a lot like guilt. I'd believed more far-fetched stories—like that my client thought he was killing a bear rather than his best friend. Many of those stories turned out to be true.

I'd also been tricked. That had been an even worse feeling, knowing the work I'd done when I believed my client was innocent had almost allowed him to get away with murder.

Now I couldn't quite seem to find the line to walk between wisdom and cynicism.

I sucked back a sigh. I'd listen. At least I could listen. I'd tell him the rule and then if what he said seemed shady, I'd hand him over to

Anderson to decide whether our firm represented him or not. Which, in the end, all depended on whether he seemed to understand and be willing to abide by our one rule.

"We have one rule here that we require all our clients to follow. You can't lie to us because we can't properly represent you if we don't know the truth."

He nodded his head again. He didn't ask about confidentiality or any of the other questions potential clients usually asked if they were guilty.

But that doesn't mean he's innocent, I reminded myself. *It's most likely just another sign that he's in shock.*

Silence hovered in the room so deeply that I imagined I could hear Jay back in my office, shifting in the chair and ruffling through papers.

Apparently, the man in front of me was going to wait for me to tell him what to do next. Of all the intakes I'd done, this was shaping up to be the strangest.

"Why don't you tell me what you do know? Starting with your name."

He looked down at his knees as if he wanted to tuck his hands between them but couldn't with them the way they were. "Nelson Burke. I'm a p-pilot." He sucked in a breath so deep it seemed like it should have split his lungs. "I got home from an international flight last night. Took some sleeping pills. With shifting time zones so much, I have a hard time sleeping when I'm home sometimes."

A touch of defensiveness entered his tone on the last bit, as if he thought we might criticize him for needing sleeping pills.

I certainly wasn't going to. "I used to need sleeping pills, too. It can help sometimes when circumstances outside your control interfere."

He stared at his hands in a way that made me think he was trying to decide whether they were really his and whether this could possibly be happening. "I had this dream where I was walking along the street and a car drove by and splashed me. Except when I woke up, I wasn't covered in water. I was covered in b-blood."

I mouth instructions to Laini to bring him a cup of coffee.

He held his hands out toward me, but kept them far enough away that I knew he didn't intend to touch me. "I don't know whose blood this is or how it got there. Your law firm was the only one I'd heard of that did criminal cases, so I looked up the address and drove here. I didn't know what else to do. The newspapers said you're the best. I know what this looks like."

He clearly thought he was innocent of whatever had happened because he couldn't remember it. It didn't mean he was. The human brain was complex and adept at self-protection. If something was too traumatic for us to handle, our brain could block it out.

He might have killed someone and then been so stricken with grief after the fact that his brain wiped out his memories.

"Will you help me?" he asked.

Anderson would like this one when he came back. "Mr. Taylor's out of town for the next two weeks. Are you comfortable signing on with our firm without meeting him first?"

Nelson's eyebrows dipped down in the middle. "You're the one I read about in the Fair Haven paper. It said you defended people who were innocent. I'd like to hire you as my lawyer."

Even I had a hard time believing that someone covered in that much blood could be innocent.

I was currently still under probation with the Attorney Discipline Board thanks to the grievance my last client filed when I managed to get him arrested on a different charge. If I took on another guilty client and had to pull a similar trick to make sure he was convicted of something, I'd be disbarred.

Technically, there was no proof—yet—that a crime had been committed. For all we knew, someone had dumped pig's blood on him as a prank while he slept.

And I wasn't grasping at straws or anything.

Nelson moved his hands toward his pajama pants, jerked them away, and rose. Laini returned with a coffee, but he waved her away and held up his hands as if to say *I shouldn't touch anything.*

He paced the floor again. "You said the one rule was that I couldn't lie to you. I'm telling you. I didn't hurt anyone."

He had come straight here instead of calling the police. That was going to look bad to them. But he could have simply destroyed his bloodstained clothes, and he hadn't. That could speak to innocence.

Or it could speak to someone smart who realized we'd think that.

Arg. I wasn't going to be guilt-tripped into taking on a client. I wasn't obligated to take on anyone as a client if I didn't want to. My autonomy to choose my own clients had even been part of the deal when I came on as partner.

But telling this man that I didn't want to personally take him on because I wasn't sure he was innocent was as good as calling him a liar. He was worked up enough without adding that to the mix.

"Mr. Burke, if I were to take on your case, you might be handed over to Mr. Taylor anyway when I go on maternity leave." I put my hand on my belly. Poor kid. I wouldn't use him or her this way once they were born. "I don't want to commit to representing you personally when I won't be able to stay for the whole case."

Could something be both a lie and not a lie at the same time?

Nelson dropped down into the chair again.

I took it as acceptance.

"I'll print off a contract," Laini said from her desk.

Nelson met my gaze again. Something in his eyes reminded me of a kicked puppy. "I'll take whatever you can give me for now, but I hope you'll reconsider. The article talked about how hard you fight for people you believe are innocent."

He didn't look at his bloodstained clothes and hands again, but I did.

"I think I'm going to need that," he said softly. "I think I'm going to need someone to believe in me. To remind me to believe in myself."

Pressure built behind my eyes. Stupid pregnancy hormones. As much as I didn't like the swollen feet, baby hiccups, and having to use the restroom every half an hour, the thing I was going to miss the least about being pregnant was my eyes' desire to tear up without my consent.

I couldn't let that convince me to commit to something now that I might regret later. He might be a master manipulator. "I'll think about it. For now, we need to get this contract signed so that you're officially represented by our firm, and then we'll decide on our next step."

He opened his mouth as if to ask what I meant by *next step*. My phone rang, interrupting whatever he'd been about to say.

Mark's picture flashed on the screen. Only minutes ago, I'd been praying for him to show up early to spare me from double-checking any more of Jay's work. Now I might have to ask him to drive around the block a few times, or go pick everyone up some muffins or donuts. He couldn't be here while we talked with Nelson.

I slid my finger across the screen, then hesitated. Somehow

saying, *Hi, husband. Could you hold off on coming to pick me up because there's a man here covered in blood?* didn't seem like the way to go.

"Nikki?" Mark's voice had the slightly distant, noisy quality of someone speaking through Bluetooth. "Are you there?"

"I'm here." First I'd find out how close he was. "Are you on your way?"

He made a negative sound. "I'm trying to find someone else to pick you up, but it might mean you have to wait a little bit. I'm sorry, sweetheart."

He didn't have to tell me why he wouldn't be picking me up. There was only one possible reason. He'd gotten called in to work.

A wait would actually be beneficial since I had to deal with—

My stomach felt too warm, like a bout of nausea coming on. I'd turned my back on Nelson to take the call. Now I sneaked a peek.

The timing felt too convenient. As county medical examiner, Mark was called in anytime someone died outside of a hospital or hospice, but what were the odds he'd get a call at the same time as a client showed up at our office, covered in blood and claiming innocence? "Suspicious death or accident?"

"Suspicious death." A note of wariness entered Mark's voice. "Why?"

"In Fair Haven?"

"Yes. Why?"

"I don't think you need to worry about finding me a ride. If I'm right about the scene you're heading to, I'll be able to get a ride with Chief McTavish."

_____

3

*M*ark's groan carried through the phone. "There's a battle going on in my mind over how much I should ask in response to that."

The urge to hug him and hold on tight hit me out of nowhere. I could blame it on pregnancy hormones, too, but it probably said more about how much I loved him. "There's not a lot I can say right now, especially if you're going to be the ME on the case. And it might not be related to what I'm working on."

I wished I could ask him the victim's name, but he wouldn't be able to tell me anything like that, either, not until the next of kin had been notified. Even then, I wouldn't be given information until and unless they decided Nelson was involved.

"Make sure you're not alone." The tenderness in Mark's tone felt like the hug I'd been craving. "Stay safe, okay?"

"I will. You too."

He chuckled. He saw more dead bodies than I did, but I somehow ended up in more life-threatening situations. Joking about it helped ease a bit of the tension for us both.

I disconnected the call.

I turned around at the same time as Nelson handed the signed contract back to Laini. The blood on his hands was dry enough that he hadn't left any smudges on the paper.

Which brought us back to the first dilemma we needed to face.

I pulled a chair up closer to his. Laini retreated back into the hallway leading to our offices, presumably to take the contract to Jay and fill him in on what was happening up here.

I sat in my chair. A bony baby part poked into me, making it hard to find a comfortable spot. Our baby had kicked like a normal baby, but he or she had also seemed to take great joy out of jabbing me with knees and elbows.

According to my mom, I'd done the same thing. Even though she wasn't someone who believed in superstitions or premonitions, she'd looked back on it as a hint that I'd become someone who would poke and prod until I got what I wanted—qualities that benefitted a lawyer.

Mark and I had agreed that we weren't going to put pressure on our child to follow in either of our footsteps. He or she could be a doctor or a lawyer if they wanted. They could also take over Sugarwood with Stacey's little Noah or teach school or fix cars in Tony's garage. If what they wanted to do was work the desk at The Sunburnt Arms bed and breakfast, we'd support them as long as they chose an honest job and worked hard at it. Mark had that freedom growing up. I hadn't.

I shifted position, but the sharp knee or elbow stayed firmly in place.

I'd have to focus on what needed to be done despite feeling like someone was stabbing me with the handle of a rolling pin.

"We need to decide what to do." I motioned toward his hands. "You can't sit around like this for much longer."

Nelson shook his head. The movement still had a slow, shell-shocked quality to it, almost like his body was reacting the way it knew it should to cues, but he wasn't entirely conscious of it. "It itches."

I choked down a laugh. Not professional or appropriate considering that was someone's blood we were talking about. The look on his face said he hadn't intended it as a joke. "I never advise a client to destroy evidence, so we're left with two choices. We could bag your clothes and wait to see if the police contact you. The downside to that is it still makes you look like you were trying to hide something and that you knew your clothes were something the police would want."

Two more head bobs from Nelson.

"Or we can proactively call the police." Even though it might mean he lost confidence in our firm and wanted to go somewhere else, I needed to tell him the whole truth. "That phone call I took was from my husband. He's the county medical examiner, and he was called in to a suspicious death. It might be whoever the blood belongs to."

Nelson's hands twitched like he desperately wanted to scrub his face with them or run his fingers through his hair. The inability to touch himself in the million ways people did every day must be even worse than the itch.

His hands stilled as if he'd forced them to come back under his control. "What would you do?"

Normally, when it came to practicing the law, the better question would be what would my parents do. In this case, I honestly wasn't sure. They'd likely advise him to go home and clean up and leave it at that. It wouldn't be directly telling him to destroy evidence, but it also wouldn't give the police an advantage. My parents never offered up anything to the police unless it benefitted them and their client in some way.

As much as I loved my parents, I wasn't them. I'd learned the hard way that—sometimes, at least—my strength as a lawyer came in the ways I was different.

"If I was innocent, I'd call the police."

I could almost hear my dad's voice in my head telling me how stupid my faith in the police was. But he almost always defended the guilty. I defended the innocent, and I believed that the police generally wanted to find the truth. That meant that, even though we were technically on opposite sides, we were still trying to reach the same end goal.

"Would you make the call? Because, well..." Nelson held up his blood covered hands again.

Since Nelson told me he lived right outside Fair Haven and the crime scene Mark had been called to was also in Fair Haven, it seemed to make sense to call the Fair Haven police department rather than the smaller force in White Cloud.

"Fair Haven PD," the voice of the new desk clerk said.

"I need to speak to either Chief McTavish or Sergeant Higgins."

"I can take a message for you if you'd like."

Of course. She didn't know my voice. She'd have no reason to put me directly through to either of them.

The baby's elbow dug into some organ this time and send a bolt of pain through my side.

I sucked in a slow deep breath. Neither Nelson nor I were in a position to sit around waiting all day for someone to call us back. "Actually, I need to talk to one of them immediately. Please tell them it's Nicole Fitzhenry-Dawes, that I have a client in my office covered in blood who needs to speak to an officer, and that whoever comes is going to need to give me a ride home."

4

*A*s we entered the police station, the new desk clerk gave me a look that said she'd been almost sure my call had been a prank right up until we came through the door. Only in both our dreams.

Chief McTavish showed me to a room where I could wait while they processed Nelson's clothes. "I would have thought that pregnancy would have kept you away from the unusual situations you tend to find yourself in."

From Russ, it would have sounded like an accusation. From McTavish, it almost sounded like teasing.

I rolled my eyes. "You can't blame me for this one. He came to me."

"You're still a magnet for it. I don't know how Cavanaugh sleeps at night." He glanced past me at the hard chairs in the room. "You'll have a wait. I'll see if I can find you something to prop behind your back."

Whether that courtesy was for my sake or Mark's or a little of both, at this point, I didn't care. Besides, once the actual questioning started, McTavish and I wouldn't be friendly anymore.

~

OFFICER PLATTEN, ONE OF FAIR HAVEN'S NEWER OFFICERS, brought Nelson to the room where I waited. Nelson had changed into a pair of blue pants and a matching blue shirt with orange across the shoulders. Prison clothes.

That outfit would have been the only thing they had to give him after taking his clothes, but it couldn't have put him at ease. It was almost as bad as pasting a big GUILTY sign on his chest.

And yet, his expression was calmer than before. More like what I would have expected from a man used to flying through storms over the Atlantic Ocean with hundreds of lives depending on him.

It was either weird or a sign of how much being covered in unidentified blood had affected him.

Hoping that blood didn't belong to a person felt more and more naïve all the time. I couldn't shake the feeling that it was also naïve of me to hope Nelson was telling the truth.

As soon as Anderson got home, I'd hand this case off to him. While I hadn't decided yet how long to stay away from work once the baby was born, I didn't need to work right until the first labor pain hit.

For now, I needed to make sure we didn't lose the case before it began. "They're going to say things with the intent of upsetting you." I kept my voice low even though no one was supposed to be listening in to any conversation we had. "If you're unsure about whether or not something could be used against you, check with me before answering."

He nodded, but it was confident and sharp this time. He looked at me with the same expression of trust that my parents' clients gave to them.

What had that article he read said about me? Mandy had framed it and hung it on the wall at The Sunburnt Arms, but I hadn't wanted to see it.

The door swung open, and Chief McTavish took a seat across the table from us, making no pretense of being on our side. Not a good sign. He always looked confident. This time he looked almost like this case was a present.

He set a file folder down on the table, but he didn't open it. Nothing about it would seem suspicious to Nelson. To me, it was like a person holding down the clip on a grenade that the pin had already been pulled out of. Maybe double-checking Jay's paperwork hadn't been so bad after all. I'd go back to it if I could.

Nelson had already told the police what he'd told me when they arrived at my office. I'd been waiting here for almost three hours, reading a mystery on my phone, since then. The wait had been so unusually long that Quincey Dornbush had gone to the café to buy me a sandwich and a bottle of water. The long wait meant McTavish was up to something.

"Do you live with anyone, Mr. Burke?" Chief McTavish asked rather than having Nelson repeat his story again.

"No, sir."

"Your wife doesn't live with you?"

My neck muscles tensed, wanting to snap my head around to look at Nelson. I held still instead. He hadn't mentioned a wife.

The fact that McTavish had told me a lot. They suspected the blood belonged to Nelson's wife.

They would have known right away, though, if the address on

Nelson's driver's license matched the address of the suspicious death Mark was attending. Chief McTavish wouldn't have been inching into it if the addresses had matched.

Something else was going on here. And once again, despite being sure that this time I knew everything there was to know, McTavish seemed to have the upper hand.

Nelson shouldn't have put the trust in me that my parents' clients put in them. My parents somehow never managed to be caught off guard. Or they managed to never look like it.

Nelson's face had gone still except for the flutter in his neck that indicated blood pumping heavily underneath his skin, like his heart was beating too hard. "My wife and I are separated. We don't live together."

Oh no.

I'd been right in the first place. The suspicious death was linked. Unless I was reading everything wrong, Nelson's wife was dead. And assuming he'd told me the truth, he didn't know it yet.

The police would assume Nelson had killed her. The husband or boyfriend was always the first suspect, even when they weren't covered in blood.

McTavish no doubt planned to reveal her death to him at some point and watch his reaction. The tactic had always seemed cruel to me. My dad said it was smart.

My dad also defended the guilty. The guilty already knew the person they'd killed was dead.

But if Nelson were innocent and his wife were dead, he'd be learning about it from someone who had no intention of softening the blow.

"How long have you been separated?" McTavish asked.

Something flickered across Nelson's face. When it cleared, his eyebrows remained slightly lower than before. "Three years."

McTavish made an mm-hmm noise. "Most couples divorce before that much time has passed."

Nelson reached toward his neck as if he were going to pull a necklace from under his shirt. His hand hit empty skin. Whatever he'd been reaching for, the police would have taken along with his clothes.

Stop letting him lead your client into a trap, my dad's voice coached in my ear. *Force him to show his hand first or call his bluff.*

I shifted in my seat enough to draw Chief McTavish's attention to me. "None of this is pertinent. My client already told you that they live apart, and that he woke with blood covering him. You should be asking him about who might have wanted to play such a malicious prank on him or who would have wanted to frame him for a crime he clearly didn't commit. He's as much a victim here as whoever that blood belongs to."

An officer I had less history with would have given me a frustrated look. McTavish didn't. His look was more resigned, almost apologetic. He knew I only defended people I believed were innocent, and he probably thought I'd been duped.

I couldn't exactly tell him that I planned to pass this case over to Anderson as soon as he returned. Given my reputation, that was as good as telling him that Nelson was guilty—whether he was or not.

"We never know what piece of information might lead us to the truth, as you well know Ms. Fitzhenry-Dawes." McTavish inclined his head toward Nelson. "Your client said he'd help us however he could to sort this out."

I wanted to drop my head onto my arms on the table. Most of

the time, the people who offered to help the police were the people who were guilty. They did it to misdirect but also to make sure they knew what was happening with the investigation. It was why McTavish had once been so suspicious of me.

Nelson couldn't have known how his words could come across. He'd probably simply meant that he'd like to know what had happened as much as they did and so he was willing to cooperate.

"Mr. Burke, as I explained, we can't figure out who would have done this without knowing more about your life. Why were you and your wife separated for so long without divorcing?"

I wanted to shout *liar* at McTavish, but that would have been unprofessional. He didn't want to know about Nelson's life to help him. He knew it. I knew it. Nelson was the only one who didn't know it.

I slid a hand slightly closer to Nelson, drawing his attention. "You don't have to answer that or anything else he asks you."

Nelson's eyes scrunched slightly. "I want to. You said that if I was innocent, I should tell them the truth, and not to let anything they asked upset me."

Heat snaked up my neck as if I'd bent over and ripped a hole in my pants, exposing my underwear.

He either really was innocent or he was cocky enough to think the police would never catch him. Or he was epically stupid. Unfortunately, I wasn't sure which one it was.

A tightness in my chest made me lean toward innocent. Innocent and maybe a little naïve. He was a pilot. That meant he likely had a great confidence in following rules and regulations and that everything would turn out if he did. He'd be used to straightforward conversation and directions.

"You took my crucifix," Nelson said. "So you can likely guess why. We're both Catholic." His voice dipped lower. "We also didn't want to divorce. We kept hoping we'd find a way to work through things."

"Then what was the cause of the separation?" McTavish asked, his tone conversational.

At times like this, I could forget we were, if not friends, at least friendly. I hated the way McTavish did this part of his job.

I wasn't guilt-free. I played people, too. I just hated to see it done like this when I was sure I knew where it was leading. And, short of walking out, I couldn't stop it.

Nelson's gaze shifted to the side, then back to McTavish. "We wanted children, but Connie kept miscarrying. When the doctor finally told us that she'd never be able to carry a baby to term, she couldn't accept it. I couldn't handle the thought of more dead babies. Every one broke us a little more. But she didn't want to give up." He shook his head. "Pretty soon every conversation came back to that. About how I didn't have enough faith. How I was stealing her dream. How I was a coward."

His voice had gone raw, and he swallowed twice then shook his head. "I'm sorry. Maybe Ms. Fitzhenry-Dawes is right. What does this have to do with anything? Connie and I were working on things. She wouldn't have dumped a cupful of blood on me while I slept."

Listening to the interrogation was like watching a video of a fatal accident that had already taken place. You wanted to stop what you knew was about to happen, but you couldn't. The event had happened, and you couldn't take it back. No matter what happened next, it wouldn't bring Nelson's wife back.

"And do you have a key to her house?" Chief McTavish asked.

I couldn't save Nelson from the news, but I could do my best to protect him from going to prison for his wife's murder. Because that's where McTavish was headed.

I tapped my finger on the table, breaking the stare-down between them. "Whether or not he has a key to his wife's house isn't relevant. My client had blood poured on him, not the other way around. You should be trying to find out who came into his house, who has a key to his house."

Nelson's face had gone pale except for his lips, making them look drawn on. "I don't need a key. She grew up here, and she never locks her door." His voice had a shake to it, and he hadn't seemed to have heard my warning. "Is Connie alright? It's not...the blood wasn't..."

McTavish pulled a photo from the file and slid it across the table. "Constance Burke was found stabbed to death in her house this morning by a neighbor."

That had to have been the death Mark was called to.

My throat burned. Just the thought of the blood...

Nelson jerked away from the table and dropped to the floor next to the garbage can. He retched into it.

Burning in my stomach joined the burning in my throat.

I swallowed hard once. Twice.

Lawyers don't throw up during an interview, Nicole, I could almost hear my mother lecturing me.

I had to pull my focus back. I had to. Because aside from embarrassing my parents from over six hundred miles away, if I threw up on McTavish, I'd never be able to face him again.

I had to focus on my work. My client.

My client who was throwing up.

Bad idea.

My client who might be innocent. Could someone force themselves to throw up without being able to take something or stick their finger down their throat? People could fake cry, fake sneeze, fake a lot of things, but I didn't think that was one of them.

Nelson sat back up. He wiped his mouth on the sleeve of the jumpsuit with the air of someone flipping the middle finger. "How dare you?" His words rasped out. "That's my *wife*."

"Your estranged wife, Mr. Burke. Half of all the murders of women that I've investigated during my career have been committed by an intimate partner. And in this case, you're the obvious choice. You can't really expect me to believe that someone broke into your wife's home and your home on the same night. Do you leave your door unlocked, too?"

The look on Nelson's face said he'd love to cuss McTavish out but that he'd learned to hold his tongue during tense situations. "They wouldn't have needed to break into my house. They'd only have needed to go through her unlocked door. She had a key to my apartment labeled and hanging on her key rack right next to where she hung her coat."

"You seem intimately aware of your wife's house for people who weren't living together."

The way McTavish continued to push settled my stomach. My parents might have been embarrassed of me if I threw up on McTavish. They'd certainly be embarrassed of me if I let him continue to badger my client.

I placed a hand on Nelson's sleeve—the still-clean one. "My client has already told you that they were working on their relationship. It's only natural that he'd have been at her house."

McTavish took the photo and slipped it back inside the folder. "Now, see, that's how I know your client is lying. We have a witness who says that Mr. Burke wanted a divorce, and his wife refused to give it to him. That doesn't sound like working on their relation-ship, but it does sound like a motive for murder."

Crap. I forced myself to keep my gaze on McTavish rather than letting it slide to Nelson. Had he lied to me after all? The smell floating through the room said he hadn't faked being sick, but perhaps there was a way to train yourself to lose the contents of your stomach on demand.

If it was possible, it'd certainly be a good way to convince people of your sincerity. Most people, anyway. McTavish might be the only person I knew who was more skeptical and suspicious of everyone than I was. Given that he used to work for internal affairs, where his job was to root out corruption and wrongdoing among people who were supposed to be the most honest and trustworthy, his cynicism made sense. He might have seen people who'd gone to even greater lengths to hide their guilt.

But Nelson's guilt or innocence only mattered if he was going to be my client long-term. He wasn't. I wasn't taking that risk. Not so close to my baby's birth. Anderson could have this case as soon as he came home.

In the meantime, I had to make sure not to snarl it up for him. "You can't expect us to believe that you found a witness that quickly."

Technically, that wasn't true, and McTavish knew it. They'd had hours now to start speaking to people who'd known Connie. Had we not called them first, one of those people would have been Nelson anyway. We'd simply fast-tracked the inevitable.

That said, witnesses who offered up information too quickly and too definitively on matters that they shouldn't have known about were sometimes trying to protect themselves. McTavish knew that, too.

Hopefully, I could buy us enough wiggle room that Nelson could walk out of here a free man for a few more days at least.

"A witness willing to comment on the status of their marriage could be mistaken, and even if they weren't, that isn't enough to arrest my client on."

"No," McTavish said. "But the blood test results are. The blood on Mr. Burke's shirt is a match for his wife."

5

My doctor gave Stacey a look when he came into the room that said he couldn't figure out who she was. We didn't look like sisters. She was obviously too old to be my daughter and too young for us to be a same-sex couple, even if he hadn't met Mark already.

He introduced himself to her and shook her hand. "And you are?"

"Stacey," she answered simply.

I licked my lips to hold in a laugh. Even though she wouldn't be a teenager much longer, Stacey still had that teenage way about her of not clarifying relationships. Somewhere once we reached adulthood, we learned that other people wanted to know how you were connected to the person standing next to you, that it made them uncomfortable when you refused to give your companion a title.

I couldn't be sure without looking straight at her, but my peripheral glimpse of Stacey's expression made me think she almost enjoyed watching the doctor's discomfort over her anonymity. She'd tilted her head forward so that her hair partly blocked her face from his view. She'd always thrived on staying off everyone's radar.

Watching suspects in a murder case squirm was one thing. I wasn't as comfortable watching it happen to my doctor. I needed this man to be confident. For all I knew, my dizzy spells meant there was something wrong with my baby. "Stacey's my good friend, and the little guy in the stroller is my godson." Noah looked around the room, ignoring all of us, a half-eaten digestive biscuit clutched in his fist. "My husband had to work, but we didn't think I should be driving. Stacey offered to be my moral and physical support."

The pinched expression left my doctor's face. "The good news is you won't need moral support. Your dizzy spells are caused by your uterus pushing on your vena cava. It's not uncommon."

Not uncommon. That phrasing always felt like waffling to me. Maybe it worked on people whose parents hadn't taught them to notice every potential flaw in an argument, but it wasn't going to slip past me as an explanation. "Does that mean it's normal or not? Because saying it's not uncommon isn't the same thing as saying it's normal."

If he could have rolled his eyes at us without looking unprofessional, he might have. "It's not normal, but it's nothing to be concerned about unless it gets worse. The inferior vena cava is what returns your blood from your lower half up to your pelvic veins and heart. When your uterus puts pressure on it, it slows the return of blood and that's why you feel dizzy. For now, you just need to avoid situations that could make it worse."

Unfortunately for me, those situations included driving, sleeping on my back, and walking for any length of time. The doctor recommended I buy a large body pillow to help me sleep on my side and that I not walk alone or drive.

He tried to make it sound like a lovely vacation and an excuse to be pampered—like every woman's dream right before she'd be spending the entirety of her days caring for a small life was to be cooped up inside her house early.

I felt a bit like Velma looked when she'd stolen food and someone took it away from her before she could finish it—a combination of grumpy and please-give-it-back.

I couldn't even take my dogs for walks in case I passed out and hit my head. Technically, I could join Mandy and Russ, but since they were now "courting"—as Mandy called it—I'd end up feeling like a third wheel. Besides, I wasn't sure I could handle Russ fussing at me the whole time about whether I should be out walking at all.

Stacey pushed the stroller out of the room ahead of me. It was a good thing she had to push Noah. At least no one could suggest that I should ride in a wheelchair from the office to the car like an invalid.

"How am I supposed to do my job?" I blurted.

Stacey glanced back over her shoulder, somehow navigating the hallways without looking. "You'll be like a celebrity with a chauffeur. Pregnancy made me want to sleep all the time. I would have loved to have someone drive me around so I could have slept on the way." She shrugged as if it all made sense, and I should have understood already. "It's the slow season right now, and Noah loves car rides, so I'll help drive you."

Stacey said it with such an easiness that she almost sounded like she'd enjoy the extra time with me. And I'd enjoy the extra time with her. The doctor might have thought we were weird because Stacey wasn't a blood relative, but we were both an only child. When I looked at her, I didn't see just an employee or a friend. I saw a little sister.

So why was this so hard for me?

My mom would say it was because I wasn't cut out to stay home. I was meant to work. She'd insisted ever since we found out I was pregnant that I should go back to work after the baby was born.

Maybe she was right. The closer I got to the birth of the baby, the less sure I was about whether I should go back to work and when I should go back to work if I did. I loved my job. I was good at what I did. I also still remembered what it felt like to be little and want my mom and have her not be there. I didn't want to put my career ahead of the well-being of my children—or have them feel that I was.

As soon as we were in the car, I dialed Mark's number. Since I'd insisted Stacey drive my car to at least save her the gas, the call connected through Bluetooth.

Mark answered as Stacey slid the parking slip into the machine and the bar lifted to allow us passage. I filled him in on what the doctor had said.

"I'm headed home, so I'll meet you there with dinner. And I have something to take your mind off of not being allowed to drive."

Only one thing could possibly cheer me up right now. "You have the autopsy report?"

"I do. You're officially Nelson Burke's counsel on record, so you're entitled to take a look."

I grinned. That was a bit of good news. At least I'd have something to think about other than my loss of freedom.

We disconnected the call.

Stacey glanced at me, then returned her gaze to the road. "You two are weird."

"Weird how?"

"Most husbands bring their pregnant wives flowers or ice cream to cheer them up. Yours brings you news about dead bodies."

ANOTHER CAR SAT NEXT TO MARK'S IN THE DRIVEWAY WHEN Stacey dropped me off. The car had a bumper sticker for an Ohio sports team alongside one that said Detroit Pistons inside a red basketball. Whoever it belonged to, they clearly weren't originally from here, but they'd been here long enough to adopt at least one Michigan team as their own. I didn't know enough about sports to know how long that would take. The only time Mark watched sports was when Grant invited him over to watch NFL games.

We hadn't been expecting anyone, as far as I knew. The only person who tended to show up unannounced was Mandy, and that wasn't her car.

I entered the house, and Velma and Toby stampeded to me. Based on the location of their dog beds to the toys, they'd been happily occupied before I got there.

"Don't you worry about them being too rough?" a man's voice that sounded vaguely familiar said from the direction of the kitchen table.

I glanced up from the ear scratches I was trying to evenly distribute. Officer Kincaid sat at the table, a cup of coffee in front of him. He wore cargo shorts and a t-shirt rather than his uniform, but I still recognized him. He'd been one of the officers to take my statement after I was nearly run down by a truck a few months ago. I would have been hit had Hal, my firm's private investigator, not pushed me out of the way.

My body tensed like my bones were trying to turn to iron.

What if the hit-and-run driver had been released on a technicality of some sort?

Mark shook his head, presumably in reply to Kincaid's question. "They've been extremely gentle with Nikki since the pregnancy. They follow her everywhere."

Marks' words registered but barely. My vision narrowed at the edges.

I sucked in a deep breath before the lack of oxygen added to my other dizzy spells. Kincaid was out of uniform. Whatever this was, it wasn't official business. Besides, if he wanted to tell me that the driver had somehow been set free, he would have called me. He wouldn't have shown up at our house out of uniform.

"I should get going now that your wife's home." Kincaid pushed to his feet. "Thanks for the coffee. I just hope you'll reconsider. So many people could benefit from your experience."

Ah, so that's what it was about. The bars of tension disintegrated from my spine.

Mark had originally been scheduled to speak at a conference this month. When we found out I was pregnant and due near to the date, he'd cancelled. The conference organizers had called again last week because the speaker they'd arranged to fill his place broke his leg and wouldn't be able to attend. They'd hoped Mark would reconsider.

Kincaid was probably Mark's biggest fan. Even though Mark chatted with him regularly on the phone about forensics, Kincaid had never been to our house. He must have heard about the situation with the conference and came to try to convince Mark to change his mind.

I gave Velma another scratch behind the ear, and she let out the roo-roo-roo that big dogs tended to make when you hit the right spot. I didn't want Kincaid to stay late, but he didn't need to run off on my account. "It's no problem if you want to stay. I haven't had the one cup of coffee I'm allowed for the day yet. I could join you."

Kincaid smiled in a way that made him look fresh-from-the-academy young. "That's okay, Mrs. Cavanaugh. I heard you're looking forward to going over an autopsy report. I wouldn't want to get in the way."

If he understood Mark's and my particular brand of couple's time, he really was a kindred spirit.

Kincaid headed in my direction, toward the door. Toby wagged his tail and plodded toward him. Any time anyone moved in the house, Toby took it as a sign that they wanted to give him attention.

The hair between Velma's shoulder blades raised. She moved her body between Kincaid and me and let out a low, hard growl.

Kincaid froze. He didn't turn pale the way most people probably would have when faced with a 125-pound dog who'd gone from affectionate to aggressive in the span of two steps. The only sign that he felt threatened were his stillness and dilated pupils.

I grabbed Velma's collar and moved sideways toward the laundry room. She came with me without resisting, but she maneuvered so her body stayed between us. She kept her gaze tight on Kincaid. The growling stopped at least.

"Sorry about that, Elijah," Mark was on his feet now too. "It's not personal. That's the other thing the dogs have started doing since Nikki's pregnancy."

I rested a hand on Velma's neck. My tension earlier couldn't have helped. Both dogs tended to read my emotions and react to them.

Talk about being a terrible hostess. Not only did Kincaid feel like he had to run off because I'd come home, but now my dog was treating him like a criminal. "She really is like this with everyone new now. She even blocked Mark for a while."

Mark shot a mock glare in Velma's direction. "I found out where her loyalties lie."

Kincaid shook out his shoulders. "You won't have to worry about anyone messing with your kid once it's born, at least."

Mark chuckled, but a shiver ran over my arms. Hopefully we never had to test that theory out. The thought of both my baby and Velma in danger...

Kincaid shook Mark's hand one more time. "You'll think about it?"

Mark glanced at me, fast like he didn't want to be caught doing it. "I'll think about it."

Kincaid might not have recognized Mark's tone, but I did. It was his not-a-chance-but-I'm-too-polite-to-say-so voice.

Kincaid turned in my direction and touched his forehead where the brim of his hat might have been. "Ma'am."

He ducked out the door before Velma changed her mind about letting him leave in one piece.

As soon as the door closed, Velma trotted back over to one of the dog beds, dropped down, and closed her teeth around a toy shaped like a giraffe.

Mark pulled me into his arms and kissed me. "At least she doesn't block me anymore."

I rested my head on his shoulder even though it required me to lean forward slightly to adjust for my belly. With all the swings of the last couple of days, being held felt good. Like I could transfer all the stress and decisions to Mark.

Kincaid's hopeful expression swam back into my mind.

This might be Mark's last chance to attend a forensic conference for a while. Once the baby came, I'd want him to stay home and help at least until we figured out a routine. "You can go to that conference if you want. It'll be your last chance for a while."

Mark shook his head, brushing against my hair. "With you not able to drive? No way."

I pulled back slightly so I could see his face. "Stacey offered to taxi me around, and you know Mandy and your mom will help, too. You'll only be gone a few days."

Mark planted a kiss on my forehead and released me. "Let's take a look at the autopsy report, and then I'll run into town and pick us up something for dinner. With your driving privileges revoked, we might as well take advantage of a take-out meal while we can."

He didn't really think I'd miss that obvious dodge, did he?

I opened my mouth to call him on it, then squished it shut again. Maybe he genuinely didn't want to go. Travel and conferences could be exhausting. With the baby coming soon, he might simply want to get all the sleep he could in advance. Kincaid was already pressuring him. He didn't need me joining in and pushing him to do something he didn't want to do.

Mark brought the file to the couch. I curled in next to him. If our child were already here, this would be a gruesome and entirely inappropriate bedtime story.

Warmth flooded my head in the way that warned me a bout of nausea was coming if I wasn't careful.

I placed my hand on top of the file before Mark could open it. "Maybe you should summarize it for me for now."

Considering I'd stood staring at a man covered in human blood a few days ago, it made no sense that my stomach would object to seeing the autopsy report. Then again, it didn't make sense that, when I entered my third trimester, I started craving olives. Olives were soft and briny and disgusting, and I'd wanted them on every-thing from pizza to subs all of a sudden. We even had a jar of the green ones in the fridge.

Pregnancy was a weird state of affairs.

Mark moved the physical copy of the autopsy report to the coffee table and looped an arm around my shoulders, pulling me closer. He rested his free hand on my belly bulge. "Hopefully you'll be able to handle listening to the results. You're going to find them interesting."

I laid a hand over his on my stomach and willed the baby and myself to stay calm. I hadn't had severe nausea since I moved into the latter stages of the pregnancy, but my queasiness continued regularly. The doctor told me that people with sensitive stomachs or people prone to stress or fatigue often continued to struggle with an upset stomach throughout pregnancy.

Mandy had given me a piece of ginger root to carry around with me. She insisted that all I needed to do was smell it whenever I felt queasy. It worked when I remembered to keep it with me. Unfortu-nately, the last time I remembered seeing it, I'd stuffed it into my purse, which I'd left by the door.

I wasn't about to go get it or relinquish my comfortable spot next to Mark so he could get it for me.

At least the baby wasn't hiccupping anymore, and if I could just get my brain to focus on the puzzle instead of the gore, I'd feel better. "Fire away."

"Official cause of death is blood loss due to a severed carotid artery."

I focused on my breathing and kept my tendency to visualize everything locked down. "That's what you expected before the autopsy."

Mark nodded. "That's not the part that's interesting. Without getting too graphic, we see specific blood spray patterns depending on the wound type, location, and proximity of the attacker. Nelson Burke was covered in blood. He didn't have a spray pattern on him."

I sat up a little against Mark, even though there wasn't a file laid out that I needed to get a better look at. "And with this type of injury, you would have expected a spray pattern, not just a glob of blood." I meant it as a question, but it came out as a statement.

"The prosecutor will likely try to argue that he stabbed her, then felt remorse and used his hands to put pressure on her wound and stop the bleeding. When that failed and he had hands covered in blood, he wiped them down his shirt without thinking clearly about it. Wiping off our hands when there's something unpleasant on them is an almost instinctive human reaction."

The counterargument sprang immediately to my mind. The amount of blood on Nelson's clothes was more than he could have gotten there by wiping off his hands.

Ostensibly, he didn't do a belly flop in her blood. If he'd fallen into it, he should have had blood on the bottom of his shoes or on his knees, and there'd been blood on neither. And he still had blood on his hands when the police took him in to process his clothes. Why wipe the blood off only to smear more on?

Besides, I knew from seeing him up-close that the blood on his shirt wasn't in a smear pattern from dirty hands, either.

None of those counterarguments were concrete enough to have the charges against Nelson dropped. No prosecutor who wanted to keep their job would drop the charges against a man who couldn't explain why he was covered in his estranged wife's blood.

My chest felt tight for a reason I couldn't put my finger on. "You think he's innocent?"

"I think he was telling the truth when he said he didn't know what happened, at the very least."

A lot like Clement Dodd, one of my former clients. Clement had, in fact, murdered someone, but he hadn't meant to. He'd done it thinking he was defending himself.

If Nelson Burke were telling the truth, he was exactly the kind of client I liked to represent. He was a man who looked guilty and wasn't. Even if he'd killed his wife, he hadn't been in his right mind at the time.

I squeezed Mark's hand, the one resting on the spot where our baby nestled in his or her water bed. "Just because he might be innocent doesn't mean I should be the one to represent him. Our baby will likely be born before his case is finished."

"You dove right into Zach Williams' case even though that could have gone on past the baby's birth," Mark said. "So I don't believe that excuse. What's the real reason you're insisting on handing this case over to Anderson?"

My heartbeat kicked up so I could hear it in my ears. I'd fought to take Zach Williams' case *for* that very reason—because it might be the last one until I stayed home full-time with our baby for a while. Because I wanted to stay home for the full length of my maternity leave, that would mean no case work for at least three months. With the Williams' case, I'd been like a person going on a last binge before starting a diet.

And Zack Williams took advantage of that.

I chewed on my bottom lip. "If Nelson is guilty, and I have to do something like I did with Zach, I'll be disbarred. Or if I can't find a way to make sure he still serves time for his crime, I'll have to live with helping a man who murdered his wife go free."

Mark's hand that was around my shoulders came up and stroked the back of my neck. "That's a valid fear, but won't that be the same for every future client?"

One of the things I both loved and hated about sharing the most intimate parts of myself with someone was when he was right and called me on the fact that I was wrong.

Every client who told me they were innocent could be lying to me. Even when I'd defended people I knew and trusted in the past, they could have been lying to me. It'd happened before.

Being tricked by my client was a risk I took when I chose to defend only the innocent. I had their word to go on. If they lied, my conscience should still be clear because I'd gone in believing in their innocence.

Not a perfect solution, but if I ever wanted to practice law again after Zach Williams' betrayal, I'd have to come to peace with it.

Easier said than done, unfortunately. Every time I thought about being in that place again—where I knew I'd contributed to setting a murderer free—I felt crushed under the weight of it.

Mark left his question hanging. He'd always been good about not pushing me when he knew I wasn't ready. How he knew I wasn't ready was a mystery in itself. He claimed he wasn't great with people. He said that was one of the reasons he'd become a medical examiner rather than a surgeon or general practitioner. But he sure understood me well enough.

He'd moved on to telling me about the prototypes that would be demoed at the conference later in the month—a potential upgrade to the current chromatology equipment that would be more sensitive to drug byproducts in a person's urine, a ramon spectroscopy technique using a laser to determine the age of bloodstains without destroying the sample, and even a machine that would hopefully allow three-dimensional CT scans to become a regular and afford-able part of autopsy procedures.

Hearing Mark geek out about lab equipment made me both want to kiss him again and picked at something in my brain.

He wasn't talking like a person who was content not attending the conference where these new forensic toys would be displayed, discussed, and perhaps even fine-tuned due to the think-tank of brains who'd be in attendance asking questions and pointing out potential flaws.

He sounded like a man who wanted to see them in person. He wanted to be part of the process to advance the techniques in his field.

His hand rubbed a soothing circle on my baby bulge while he talked. I glanced down at the motion. We'd never talked about exactly why he'd cancelled his trip to this conference. I'd still be weeks away from my due date at the time, and according to every member of the Cavanaugh clan, first babies were usually late.

But Mark's first baby—the daughter who hadn't lived—hadn't been late. She'd been early. And he'd been away at a conference when it happened.

I stopped his hand. "Your turn. The conference?"

He glanced down at my belly and then away, but the motion gave him away. I'd been right, too.

"Maybe we should both face our fears," I said softly.

His arms clenched around my side. "I don't like to make the same mistakes twice."

Intellectually, he knew he couldn't have saved his first daughter. But his first wife had thought he could have. It'd broken them. Her grief had eventually led to her killing herself.

That was the part that he wished he could change. Had he been there, even if he couldn't have saved his daughter, his wife wouldn't have thought things would have been different had he stayed home.

"We have to trust that God's in control."

Mark's head moved almost imperceptibly in a nod. "I'll go if you take the lead on Nelson Burke's case. We face our fears together?"

I swiveled in his arms and kissed him on the cheek. Sometimes I still couldn't believe that we'd both found joy in the ashes of the sadness we'd faced. "Together."

6

*M*ark texted me before noon the next day to say he'd called the conference organizers. They'd already filled the presenter's spot, but they wanted him to come anyway and be on a panel on the challenges of forensic detection of certain poisons.

I texted back a smiley face and a heart.

And then there was nothing left for me to do other than call Nelson Burke and tell him that I'd be remaining on as lead in his case even after Anderson returned.

Well, that and confirming with him that he and his wife were trying to work things out. I'd lain awake longer than usual last night trying to adapt to sleeping on my side with the full-body pillow Mark and I had purchased when we went out to grab dinner. It'd given me time to consider Nelson's case.

Topping my mental list of things that didn't add up were the blood on his clothes and the witness who told the police Nelson wanted a divorce but Connie wouldn't give it to him. We didn't have any leads as to how the blood got on his clothes other than that someone set him up. That person could well be the same person who'd lied about the status of Nelson and Connie's relationship.

I dialed Nelson's number.

He picked up almost instantly. "Is there anything new from the police?"

He'd skipped the hello and gone straight to enough-hope-to-hurt-my-heart. He clearly had no idea how this worked. Now that he'd been charged with Connie's murder and was out on bail awaiting the next steps in his case, the police weren't looking for any other suspects. The prosecutor would be using the police and the other resources at their disposal to amass evidence against Nelson, but it'd all be focused on solidifying their case against him. They wouldn't be looking at the evidence from an objective viewpoint anymore.

Nelson's experience with investigations was likely limited to aviation accidents. I wasn't sure how investigators operated when there was an aviation accident, but they likely came at it differently than the police. They weren't looking for a villain. They were trying to reconstruct what happened.

This wasn't that.

Maybe it was my maternal instincts already kicking in, but I couldn't bring myself to bluntly burst his hope bubble.

"I'm starting to review all the evidence against you to build our defense." Since he seemed to assume I'd be working on his case, I didn't need to explicitly tell him I was staying on as lead. Considering how he'd reacted to McTavish's interrogation the other day, I also wanted to come at this carefully. We were in the stage where it was important that I build his trust in me. "I need to confirm one quick thing with you. Sometimes I'll need to ask you a question that you've already answered to confirm things. It's not a questioning of your integrity."

"Okay," he said in a tone that indicated he wasn't quite sure he believed me but he had no other choice than to go along.

"You and your wife both wanted to reconcile?"

"Yes." His answer was firm and quick.

"Had you ever spoken to a lawyer about divorce proceedings?"

"Never. I might not have attended mass as faithfully as Connie, but I still live the teachings of the Church. Our diocese teaches that divorce should only happen in cases of adultery, abuse, or abandonment. None of those applied."

That at least meant there weren't half-signed divorce papers lying around somewhere, waiting to disrupt our case at the worst possible moment. It didn't mean there might not be some physical evidence. He might have only casually mentioned it in passing or in an email.

If he had, hopefully he would remember to whom. Then we'd be down to one of three options. They were innocently speaking to the police because they thought Nelson had been serious about it, they had a grudge against him and wanted to harm him but hadn't played a role in Connie's murder, or they were the one who framed him because they committed the murder. "Did you speak to anyone about divorce?"

"Not even in therapy. I love...loved Connie."

My throat tightened. That shift from present to past tense had to be one of the things I hated most about dealing with death. "You can still love her. You'll see her again one day."

He cleared his throat. Twice. "Is there anything else?"

"Not for today. I'll keep you informed."

I disconnected the call.

Before I'd decided to represent Nelson myself, I'd had him write down a list of friends and family who knew Connie well. They were people we'd need to interview for leads. They could confirm what Nelson and Connie's relationship was like. They could also tell us if Connie had been acting strangely or if they knew of anyone who might want to hurt her.

I'd passed off the out-of-town part of the list to Jay since those people were the least likely to be suspects themselves. Knowing Jay, he'd be far enough into that list by now to be able to either confirm Nelson's story about not wanting a divorce or call it into question.

I called our firm, and Laini put me through to his office.

"I finished talking to everyone on the list yesterday." Jay's tone of voice almost begged for a pat on the head.

I thanked him. "What did they say about Nelson and Connie's marriage?"

Most of the out-of-town names were family—both sets of parents, some siblings, and a cousin who Connie visited for a week every winter.

"Varying degrees of what a good couple they'd been and how dedicated they still were to each other. Mr. Burke's brother must have figured out why I was asking, because he told me directly that Mr. Burke would have mentioned it to him if he was considering asking Connie for a divorce." Jay's voice shifted, letting a touch of embarrassment in. "Mr. Burke's brother sounded angry at me for even suggesting it."

Jay must think it showed failure on his part that someone knew we were digging around to find a possible motive for Nelson. What he didn't realize is that the police might have gotten there before him, setting Nelson's brother on edge.

"Some people will be offended by our questions. What did they say about anyone who might have had a grudge against Connie?"

"Nothing there, either, I'm afraid."

That left me back around where I started with the witness who lied to the police. I needed his or her name.

Once the discovery package came, I'd have all the information the police and prosecutor had. Divulging everything ahead of time so that we could prepare a defense was part of the American legal system.

Unfortunately, with how slowly the justice system worked anymore, receiving that package might cost us weeks that I couldn't afford to spend idle. If I was taking responsibility for this case, then I wanted to work on it as much as possible before the baby came.

I had to go to the source.

When Nelson stood in my office covered in blood, I'd called the front desk at the Fair Haven police station instead of calling any of the officers directly. I'd wanted a clear trail to show that we were trying to be above-board.

I could approach this more directly now. The name of the witness who claimed Nelson wanted a divorce was information I'd get eventually, after all.

I put Chief McTavish's number into my phone. If Stacey had thought that Mark cheering me up with an autopsy report was odd, she'd likely think the same was true of me having the chief of police's direct line saved as a contact in my phone.

"McTavish," he answered.

"It's Nicole."

McTavish's trademark long-suffering sigh filled his end of the phone. "I recognize your voice Ms. Fitzhenry-Dawes."

The name by which McTavish chose to address me acted as a bit of a barometer for his mood. Today, I was a lawyer, an opponent.

My mom's advice about the need to sometimes remove the rocks from the path you wanted to walk on rang in my mind.

"I'm sure you're busy, and I know I tend to take up a lot more of your time than I should." Hopefully that wasn't putting the buttering-up on so thick that he'd notice it. "I just need the name of the witness from the Burke case. The one who told you that Mrs. Burke wouldn't give her husband a divorce."

The sound of keys clicking continued on McTavish's end as if he'd been working on something and hadn't bothered to stop when he answered the phone. "That'll be in the discovery package, as you well know."

He didn't call me Ms. Fitzhenry-Dawes again, so maybe that meant I'd struck the right balance. "The thing is that I might already be on maternity leave when it comes." Nope. That wasn't going to work. McTavish would make some comment in return about how he'd be able to get more work done for a few months. This had to be about something else. "My law partner will have to handle all our cases with only a rookie law student graduate to help him. I'd like to take as much of the load off of him as I can before that happens."

Another sigh. More resigned this time. "Fine." The clicking of a mouse now. "Do you have a pen and paper? I'm not going to repeat myself."

No, of course I didn't. I scooted off the kitchen chair and grabbed the grocery list off the fridge. We'd bought a list and pen combo in the hope that making sure we had both a writing instrument and paper close by would help us avoid our tendency to let our fridge run empty without a record of what we needed to replace.

"Go ahead."

"The witness's name is *Father* Earnest Napier. He's a priest at Holy Cross Catholic Church in White Cloud."

I quickly put my phone on speaker and scrolled through the notes I'd made in my conversation with Nelson about who Connie's friends and family in the area where and where she worked. Holy Cross was the church where she worked on the janitorial staff.

McTavish rattled off Father Napier's phone number and the address of the church, but I already had it from Nelson.

I ended the call and scrubbed my hands over my face.

Of course. Because it wasn't enough that this case already involved a murderer who'd gathered the victim's blood, sneaked into Nelson's home, and planted it on him. Now it had to include a priest. How was I supposed to even begin proving that a priest was a liar?

How was I supposed to make myself want to?

7

*W*hy did the witness have to be a priest?

I sunk down onto my couch and squirmed around until I was resting on my side. My feet ached almost as much as my head, and propping my feet up often brought on a dizzy spell anymore. No doubt the doctor would tell me it had something to do with the angle it put my uterus in comparison to my vena cava nerve.

This wasn't the kind of complication or challenge that I liked in a case.

Even my parents would be calling for a strategy conference after that piece of news, though for an entirely different reason. If they knew they would be facing a priest as a witness, they'd want to select jurors with no religious affiliation.

For me, the issue ran deeper than an added challenge during jury selection. Even before I became a Christian, I'd never liked the way TV, movies, and even some books seemed to cast people of faith as either a villain doing horrible things in God's name or a secret hypocrite who was pious on the outside and acting like everyone else behind closed doors. What the media showed didn't accurately represent the Christians I'd met. It didn't accurately represent me or Mark.

Now, I was going to have to become just like one of those TV cops and accuse a priest of breaking two of the Ten Commandments or I was going to have to believe that Nelson had lied to me after all. If he had, he was probably guilty.

Neither option made me feel good about working this case.

Then again, if someone who was supposed to be a man of God had lied and murdered and done who knew what else, maybe I was the best person to bring that to light because of my own faith. I wouldn't be going after him with a vendetta to prove that a Christian was actually a bad person and therefore Christianity had to be false. I'd be seeking only the truth.

Unfortunately, before I could do anything about it, I needed to find a ride to White Cloud.

"DO YOU WANT ME TO BE YOUR BACKUP LIKE BOOTH TO BONES, OR do you want me more as a sounding board like Watson to your Sherlock?" Mandy asked an hour later as we neared the church.

The newspapers had released enough details about Connie's murder and Nelson's arrest that Mandy had come up with a whole slew of theories she wanted to talk over while we drove. The one she believed most was that Nelson had actually killed his wife, but he'd been sleepwalking when it happened.

She'd read a news story once about a man near Toronto, Canada, who drove ten miles and killed his in-laws. He had no memory of it afterward and a history of sleepwalking. But the reason Mandy thought that's what had happened to Nelson was that the Canadian man went to the police station to tell them that he had cuts on his hands and no idea how they got there.

It was in 1987, she'd said, *so there's precedent you can use when arguing for your client. You should ask if he's been diagnosed with sleepwalking.*

I didn't have the heart to tell her that Canadian court cases wouldn't carry any weight in an American court of law. International cases weren't supposed to be factored into decisions in the U.S. Though if I'd been even a little more like my parents, I would have dug into American cases involving sleepwalking, and that's the defense I would have built.

But my parents didn't care about the truth, only about winning. I'd decided long ago not to practice that way.

Mandy parked the car next to the few others already sitting in the church parking lot and looked at me expectantly, like a cadet awaiting her orders on her first day on the job.

I couldn't let Mandy come inside with me. She'd barge in, announcing who I was and asking questions that would make it obvious we suspected someone there of being the real killer.

"What I really need is for you to stay with the car." I unbuckled and pointed to my belly. "You'll need plausible deniability if Russ asks you what we did today. You can't tell him you helped pregnant me interview potential murderers."

Mandy pulled a book out of her oversized purse. "You're right. I don't want to spend all evening listening to a lecture on why you shouldn't be trundling around meeting with murderers anymore." She pressed the buttons that controlled the windows, and they slid down. "And I'm at a good spot in this story. Besides, I don't know anything about being a Catholic. I'd probably give us away."

I smiled at her and climbed out of the car before she had a moment to consider whether I knew anything about the Catholic Church, either. I knew that the preachers were called priests, and they couldn't marry. I knew Catholics were Christians. Beyond that, I couldn't have filled in even one item on a list of how they differed from the Baptist church Mark and I attended.

Except for the building. Our church was a squatty brown building that used to belong to the Rotary Club. The church in front of me was brick and nearly twice the height of a two-story house. A bell tower climbed even higher on one side, and all the windows were stained glass.

The one on the very front was a circle in purples, blues, and reds, whose design reminded me of a flower. Below it were four individual panels depicting people I couldn't identify, except for a woman holding a child with a halo around his head. That one had to be Mary and baby Jesus.

The sign in front of me on the grass confirmed that this was the right church. Holy Cross Catholic Church.

Underneath the church's name and the dates and times for the monthly blood drive and daily mass, the sign said…

What do you call a sleepwalking nun?

A roam'n Catholic.

I pulled out my phone, snapped a picture, and texted it to Mandy back in the car.

Her response was almost immediate. *Do you think it's a sign?*

I started to type *Look out your window.*

Then I realized she hadn't meant a physical, standing-on-the-front-lawn sign. She'd meant a sign that this was where we'd find the murderer because it talked about someone sleepwalking.

Instead of sending a response to her, I texted the sign to Mark.

Knowing that he worked with death all day, it was fun to lighten up his day any way that I could.

Would our child share our corny sense of humor, or would he or she groan at us and be embarrassed? I'd never been embarrassed by my parents, but my upbringing hadn't exactly been normal.

An uncomfortable tightness wound its way through my chest and down into my stomach. I still didn't have the wife part of my life figured out, and now Mark and I were about to be parents. My mom and dad believed they'd done an excellent job raising me, and in a lot of ways, they had. I'd always been safe. I'd lived a very privileged upbringing where I'd never had to worry about physical needs. But they also hadn't been there when I was sick or scared or hurt. Their jobs had been so important that I ended up feeling like more of a distraction than a wanted addition to their lives.

Whatever I did as a mom, I didn't ever want to leave our baby feeling that way.

"Excuse me," a woman said from behind me. "Is the blood drive today?"

My brain stuttered back into the present and what I was supposed to be doing. I glanced at her and back at the sign. The date was definitely yesterday, not today. "I think you missed it, but it looks like they'll post next month's date here."

The woman mumbled something about hating when calendars put Monday as the first day of the week instead of Sunday because it meant she kept missing appointments. She walked off, passing Mandy's car on her way.

Mandy's head was bowed over her book, but I'd better hurry or she'd start to wonder why I wasn't already inside. I could worry about what kind of a mom I'd be later. Right now, I needed to stay focused on being a lawyer.

The doors of the church were a heavy wood, and I had to lean back a bit to get them to open.

The inside was even more different from my church than the outside had been. Wooden pews ran in two rows, with an aisle up the center. The lights were dimmed slightly, and a tiered rack of votive candles sat at the back, in front of a statue. About half of them were lit, making the ornate holders glow red and yellow. Off to the side, nearer the front, was what looked like a small square building with three doors.

A handful of people sat in the pews, most of them older. During the workday, the church probably wasn't as busy as at other times. When I'd called ahead to ask what hours their church was staffed, the woman who'd answered had sounded confused and told me their doors were always open. That'd seemed strange to me, but it made sense now. The sanctuary here seemed like a very soothing place to pray.

"May I help you?" a man's voice whispered from beside me.

I jumped slightly and spun around. Great. I'd been caught gawking or daydreaming twice now. I was losing my edge. I blamed the lack of sleep from trying to learn to sleep on my side, wedged between Mark and my new body pillow.

The man next to me seemed to be around my age, but quite a bit taller. He wore a long black robe-style garment buttoned down the front, with a strip of stiff white fabric around the collar.

He had to be a priest, based on his clothing, but priests should definitely not be that good looking. He could have been modeling underwear rather than preparing sermons. Even his hair was styled with gel. He was a bit too polished for my personal taste, but he seemed like the type of priest whose presence could cause trouble among the younger female members of the congregation.

Or, perhaps, hiring such a young, handsome priest had been a strategic move. It would certainly encourage younger female congregants to attend faithfully.

Oi, now I sounded like Mandy with her matchmaking and conspiracy theories.

"Are you here for confession?" the priest asked, reminding me I hadn't answered his first question yet.

Getting a confession from Father Napier would be great, the sarcastic part of me wanted to say. *Then I can go home and take a nap.*

But I was pretty sure that wasn't what he meant when he said *confession* any more than the billboard out front had been what Mandy meant when she asked about a *sign*. This place was pun and double meaning heaven.

Focus, Nik. The sooner you finish here, the sooner you can have that nap.

If I chose to go back to work after the baby was born, I might be giving myself that particular pep talk a lot.

"I'm actually here to speak to Father Napier."

The young priest nodded. "You have the right day. He's the priest taking confession. There are a few people waiting ahead of you." He motioned to the people in the pews who were sitting close to the small indoor building-thing with the three doors that I'd noticed before. "But it shouldn't be too long."

Not exactly what I'd meant. "How long will he be taking confessions?"

"Another hour. You have time if you need to run an errand and come back."

The man was almost too accommodating, though perhaps that was a character trait that helped if you planned to dedicate your entire life to service. Short of bluntly telling him I was here to talk to Father Napier about his testimony in a murder case, though, it also meant I wasn't going to make much progress.

I couldn't wait an hour for Father Napier to finish hearing confessions. Mandy would definitely have come into the church by then, expecting that I was in trouble and needed help.

She wouldn't be subtle about it, and that might push Father Napier into a corner where he refused to admit that he'd even spoken to the police. After all, it would look like he'd shared information that had been told to him in confidence, via his role as a priest. Even a rumor of that could have repercussions for the reputation of the church and his place there. With as little as I knew about the Catholic Church, I did know that priests were bound by even stricter rules than lawyers were when it came to confidentiality.

I couldn't take the moral high ground and say I'd never put pressure on someone to confess to doing something like that. Truth was, I would if it meant finding the truth. But I didn't feel right doing it to a priest until I had a better idea of what was going on. For all I knew, he'd told the truth as he knew it. It was possible Connie had told him that in order to cover up some wrongdoing of her own, though I couldn't imagine what lying about her husband wanting a divorce would hide.

So unless I wanted to risk Mandy causing a scene, or unless I wanted to try to find someone else to drive me back another day, waiting wasn't an option.

If the confessions were supposed to stay private, though, that meant I had another option. I could pretend to be a parishioner and use the privacy of the confessional to speak with Father Napier.

"I'll stay," I said to the younger priest and took a spot on the pew behind the other people who the younger priest had indicated were waiting.

I didn't make eye contact with any of the other people waiting or try to make conversation, even though it would have been helpful to find out if any of them knew Connie. My parents and many other people might have looked at it as part of the job to disrupt the sanctuary to get their business done, but I wanted to respect why all these people were here. The woman who sat in front of me methodically shifted beads on a chain, and her lips moved without sound, as if she were praying.

The people waiting in front of me took varying amounts of time in the confessional. Some left directly afterward, while others moved to a different part of the sanctuary. The private nature of confession also meant that I couldn't see what they were saying or doing once they went inside. I couldn't even copy them in an attempt to appear Catholic.

And maybe that was for the best. What I was doing was already borderline sacrilegious and disrespectful. Hopefully God would forgive me because my motives were good. I didn't want to disrupt this place of worship or cause unnecessary hardship to anyone here who was innocent in Connie's murder.

One of the confessional doors opened. The woman who came out had mascara smeared under her eyes.

I glanced behind me. Thankfully, no one else seemed to be waiting at the moment. I might have chickened out if there had been.

I closed the confessional door behind me and wriggled my way down onto the small chair that waited inside. The room was tinier than an old-fashioned telephone booth. A single light on the ceiling lit it with a dim glow. It smelled a bit like Pine Sol and sweat.

How was I supposed to talk to the priest?

A little door in the wall next to me slid open. A thick wire grate separated me from the outline of the man on the other side. All I could tell about him from this angle was that he had a large nose and double chin.

"Father Napier?" my voice sounded strangely small, like the walls ate the sound. Sound proofing?

"Is this your first confession, child?" The man's voice was kind.

Apparently, I'd already made some snafu that gave it away. Catholics likely had something they said when they entered or some system they followed that I knew nothing about.

Since I'd already blown my cover, slim as it'd been, I might as well move right into what I'd come here for so that I didn't take more of the father's time away from people who were actually here to confess sins.

"I've never confessed before. I came in here because I wanted to talk to you about Connie Burke and what you told the police."

The priest shifted so that I faced him head on through the portal rather than looking at his profile. In the hazy light, I could just make out his broad face and the beginning of a sagging to his cheeks that would make him look like he had jowls. He was probably nearing fifty.

"I'm assuming you're not Catholic since no good Catholic would dishonor the nature of the confessional in this manner." All the patience and softness were gone from his voice. "Confessionals aren't intended for reporters to interview subjects. They're meant for people trying to return to right standing before God. I'd recommend you leave now."

My tongue felt like it dried to a stub inside my mouth. I wanted to explain to him that I hadn't meant any disrespect. I wanted to explain to him that I was a newer Christian, and I'd never even been inside a Catholic church before. Maybe I would need to do penance or something to make up for coming here like this.

But I didn't say any of that because, for all I knew, this was a protective action by the man who'd actually murdered Connie. Why else would he have lied to the police? Lying, as far as I knew, was a sin.

Instead of all the things that first popped to my mind, I said, "I'm not a reporter. I'm Nelson Burke's attorney."

"The title may be different, but the sentiment remains. This is neither the time or the place."

The priest's form moved again, reminding me a bit of a shadow reflected on the wall. I couldn't see his expression, and his voice gave nothing away about whether he was worried by me asking questions or not. Interviewing witnesses and potential suspects from professions that required them to hide their emotions—like doctors or counselors—always made my job harder. I had to depend on small tells. In this case, I couldn't see those either.

Even though it made me feel grimy, I couldn't give up yet. I'd dragged Mandy all the way out here, and I wanted to believe Nelson told me the truth about his relationship with Connie.

Plus, the disparity between Father Napier's story and Nelson's story was the only lead I currently had. I had to at least try to figure out if it was a viable lead or not by getting a better read on his reaction. Was he upset more because I was asking about Connie or more because I chose to do it in the confessional?

"I thought speaking privately would be better since I didn't know if what you shared was something Ms. Burke told you within the confidence of the confessional."

"If it had been, I wouldn't have told the police about it. I take the seal of confession seriously and believe that it extends even after death. I told them only what the police asked and which I was at liberty to share."

Gah, this was frustrating. He was so professional. It made me want to stamp my foot in a completely *un*professional way.

But I was a grown-up and soon to be a mom. I couldn't go around stomping my feet when I didn't get my way. All I could do was persist.

This time I'd try a leading statement. Sometimes I could learn from the way people answered them because they weren't a question. Without a question to give the respondent a direction, interesting tidbits could come out of their subconscious. "You must have known Connie well to know things about their marital situation that others didn't."

"Connie was a regular attendee and employed on our janitorial staff."

In other words, *I knew her in a professional capacity.*

The implication scratched at the back of my neck like ill-fitting clothing. A professional relationship wouldn't explain it.

Nelson and Connie's family claimed divorce wasn't on the table. If Connie hadn't told her family, then it logically must have been something Connie told Father Napier in an official private capacity. Or it had to be a lie she told him openly for some reason we hadn't yet figured out.

Assuming Nelson *didn't* want a divorce, Connie had either lied to Father Napier or Father Napier had lied to the police, and by extension, was lying to me now.

"Since this isn't an appropriate time or place"—I tried to infuse humility into my voice. It wasn't hard, since I did feel bad if I'd violated some sanctity that I shouldn't have—"then maybe we can make an appointment to talk further. I would have done that for today, but I was told the church is always open. I didn't tell the receptionist why I was calling, and I guess she misunderstood."

"What's your name?"

Strange question. Surely he wasn't going to write me into his appointment book on the spot. Did priests keep their appointments on phones? Only one way to find out. "Nicole Fitzhenry-Dawes."

"I'm sure your intentions are good, Ms. Fitzhenry-Dawes, but there's nothing else I can tell you that I didn't already tell the police. I'm very sorry."

He slid the door between us shut. Even though it was impossible, I would have sworn I felt the confessional shudder with the force.

_a_fter spending the ride back to Fair Haven with Mandy grilling me and suggesting all kinds of ways I could have tricked him into telling me more information, from pretending to be Connie's ghost ("I don't think priests believe in ghosts," I'd replied) to planting a bug in his office (which I'd informed her was illegal), I almost didn't have any energy left to think about the case, let alone plan my next step.

I knew what I needed to do next. I needed to talk to Connie's close friends who lived locally and see if she'd told any of them the same things she'd told Father Napier. If she hadn't, then it would confirm that Father Napier was lying.

If she had, then either Nelson should be a professional poker player based on his bluffing skills alone or Connie had chosen to lie about their situation for some reason.

The problem I'd created for myself in taking Mandy with me today was that she wanted to be my assistant every day. She'd even asked me to tell her when I'd need her next so she could schedule the rest of her staff to give her the day off.

I wasn't always going to be able to find graceful ways to keep her exuberance under wraps. It was one of the things I loved about her. It was one of the things that made her an excellent bed and breakfast owner.

And it was one of the things that made her unsuited to navigating tricky situations in murder cases.

I fell asleep before I could decide what to do and woke up when Mark came home. It took an act of will to keep from simply pulling one of the homemade lasagnas from the freezer that his mom had put there to help after the baby was born. Instead, we opted for simple chicken Caesar salads, but at least it gave me an idea of how to handle Mandy. She'd offered to also help create some easy freezer meals for us.

I texted her to set up a time when we could get together for that, telling her I needed that help more than a sidekick in crime fighting. If there was anything Mandy loved more than a good mystery, it was cooking.

Unfortunately, that left me in need of a driver. I could interview Connie's friends over the phone, but a phone call stripped away the body language and facial expressions that often told me more than the words people spoke.

"Why not hire Hal to go with you again?" Mark said. "I'm sure he won't be scared away by the hit-and-run."

I snorted. No, Hal—the private investigator our law firm preferred to use—wouldn't refuse to play bodyguard or chauffer for me just because the last time he'd been hired for that particular role, he'd ended up in the hospital. He was former military. He took risks and injury as part of the job. "He planned a vacation for his family, too, when he heard Anderson would be gone for two weeks."

"Then a lot of your cases should be on hold. What about the

new lawyer? He might learn something from following you around."

That would be the mature thing to do. Working for our firm was Jay's first job post-graduation and licensing. I'd have to allow him to expense the extra drive time, but that was fine. If Anderson had a problem with it, I'd simply cover it myself. It'd still be less expensive than hiring Hal to follow me around would have been.

"Jay it is."

THE NEXT DAY WAS SATURDAY, BUT JAY SAID HE HAD NO PROBLEM coming in to work. He'd known when he took the job that it could mean odd hours when a case demanded it. If we wanted to speak with possible witnesses in person rather than depending on the phone, evenings and weekends were often a necessity.

He came prepared with the address I'd texted him already put into his GPS. According to Nelson, Connie's closest friend was her widowed next-door neighbor. The two had connected over the additional challenges of being a woman living alone.

The fact that Nelson had known that detail made me think again that he was telling me the truth. The voice of uncertainty in my head tried to tell me that my increased confidence was proof Nelson was lying to me. It'd been a long time since I'd felt this unsure of myself and my ability to read people.

But I was not going to be the one who gave up. Mark had suffered a worse tragedy than I had, and he was still facing up to his fears and going to the conference. Part of marriage was supposed to be encouraging each other to be the best possible versions of ourselves. I couldn't help Mark do that for himself if I wasn't going to let him do that for me, too.

Connie lived in one of the older, more established sections of Fair Haven, not far from the McTavishes. This section of town had well-kept but not ostentatious homes and was well away from the tourist areas.

Despite how close her home was to Sugarwood, it took us almost as long to get there as it would have taken to drive back to the church in White Cloud. Jay, apparently, felt that pregnant women—or, more specifically, pregnant bosses—needed to be driven around at ten miles an hour under the speed limit.

When we finally reached the right street, Connie's house was easy to spot because the front door was locked with a large generic police lock and crime scene tape surrounded the yard.

"Arriving at destination, on the right," the GPS's stilted female voice said.

Jay eased the car to a stop so slowly that I almost didn't feel the movement actually cease. He jumped out, ran around, and opened my door for me. You'd think we were on a first date or that I was carrying his baby.

The house we'd parked in front of didn't have a number on it. At least, not a complete number. The starting 2 was still there, but whatever had been behind it had long ago fallen off and not been replaced. The front porch overall looked like it needed a fresh coat of varnish, and the flower gardens had the wilted appearance of plants that should have been watered but instead had been left to fend for themselves with whatever rain fell.

It didn't quite fit with the rest of the houses on the street. Nelson had said that Ms. Tan was widowed, so perhaps this was just a sign that she was struggling to maintain her home on her own. I'd noticed the positive change when Mark and I got married. Two people working as a team could complete so much more than one person trying to do it all on their own.

Jay glanced at me as if he wasn't sure whether to offer his arm like a gentleman in an old-time movie or not. I slipped past him and headed up the sidewalk, leaving him to trail along at my heels.

I rang the doorbell.

The woman who answered opened the wooden door, but not the screen door in front of it. She had thin blonde hair that looked like it'd been dyed one too many times and hollows under her eyes. A little boy of three or four walked by in the hallway behind her, eating straight from a box of chocolate chip cookies. Not exactly the most nutritious meal.

The woman glanced from me to Jay and swore. "Ain't it enough you poked through my house last week, you gotta come again." Her words had a clumsy quality to them, not slurred, exactly, but headed in that direction. "You'd think you'd figure out by someone killing her that she was just trying to start trouble."

The *she* that someone killed had to be Connie, but whoever this woman was, she didn't seem to be expecting us. Based on what she'd said and the glimpse I got of the little boy, my guess would be she thought we were social workers. "Ms. Tan?"

She pursed her lips. "Other side."

And slammed the door in our face.

I turned around. Jay stood on the second step. He looked like someone had bleached his face.

"I'm so sorry, Mrs. Fitzhenry-Dawes. The GPS—"

I held up my hand. "It's not a big deal. All it means is we need to walk two houses down."

I waited for him to move out of my way so I could descend the stairs, and we headed back the way we'd come, him still trying to apologize.

In his interview, Jay had seemed eager to please. Anderson had liked that about him. He thought it would let us mold Jay to fit our practice rather than hiring a lawyer with more experience. Now, though, I was starting to think Anderson might regret that decision. Jay wasn't just eager to please. He was almost unable to function independently.

Maybe it was good I was here working with him rather than Anderson. I probably had more patience for that than Anderson would have. I knew what it was like to doubt your abilities.

Ms. Tan's yard was more what I'd expected. Even in September, her grass was green. Her gardens had a little wildness to them, but in a way that made them more appealing.

She waved to us and stepped outside as we came up the walkway. "I saw you pull up and head to the wrong side. There wasn't anything I could do to stop you."

Ms. Tan was the opposite of her near neighbor. Instead of the other woman's height and blonde hair, she was short, dark-haired, and looked like at least one of her parents was of Asian descent. I hadn't traveled that part of the world enough to be able to tell what country she was from, and I didn't want to insult her by asking, especially since, given her unaccented English, she'd probably been born here and was as American as I was. If someone was judged on their family heritage rather than where they were born, then I should be called Scottish and British rather than American.

Ms. Tan motioned to a patio set. A pitcher of lemonade sat on the small table along with three glasses. "I thought we could meet out here since we don't have many nice days left."

Had she been someone I was considering as a suspect, I might have thought she was trying to hide something by keeping us outside. But according to Nelson at least, Amie Tan was more like Connie's sister after over ten years living as neighbors. When Connie and Nelson separated, Nelson had been the one to move out. Connie had stayed in their original home, with the intent that he'd move back in once they settled their differences.

I slowly lowered myself down into one of the seats. The additional challenge in sitting and standing up with a belly the size of a birthday helium balloon was something no one warned you about.

Ms. Tan sat next to me. The skin surrounding her eyes was red up close, and despite her careful makeup, her face still looked puffy. Connie hadn't been gone very long. Crying was probably still part of each day for her. It would have been for me had I lost Stacey or Elise or Mandy. Even now, with my Uncle Stan having been gone almost two years, I still struggled sometimes when I thought about him. Especially now, when I desperately wanted to be able to introduce him to my baby once he or she was born.

I accepted the glass of lemonade Ms. Tan offered me. "Thank you for meeting with us. Friends and family of victims sometimes don't want to meet with defense counsel, and that makes it more difficult for us to uncover the truth."

Ms. Tan ran her pinky finger over the frosty side of her own glass. "I don't believe Nelson did this. He should be acquitted. Then the police will have to go back to looking for the real killer."

Thank goodness I wouldn't have to fight an uphill battle this time the way I had so many times before. "You told the police you weren't home the night it happened."

She sipped her lemonade as if her mouth would be too dry for her to answer without wetting it first. "My aunt fell and broke her hip a month ago. Tuesdays and Thursdays are my nights to sleep at her house in case she needs anything."

So Ms. Tan hadn't been away at random. That suggested whoever had killed Connie either knew Ms. Tan's schedule because they knew Connie and Ms. Tan personally, or they'd been observing Connie's neighborhood in preparation. Whatever this murder was, it wasn't unpremeditated. Unfortunately, even the implication of prior knowledge like that could cause trouble for Nelson's defense.

I pushed away the tiny seed of doubt it also wanted to plant in my mind about his innocence. Ms. Tan thought he was innocent, and she'd known the Burkes much better than I ever would. "What makes you sure it wasn't Nelson?"

Once the question came out, it hit my ears as potentially confrontational, but hopefully she'd understand that wasn't the intent since I was Nelson's lawyer.

She took another sip and looked like she was rubbing the liquid around in her mouth. "No man who wants to murder his wife comes every Saturday to mow her lawn and empty her mouse traps."

A smile tugged at my lips. No, they probably didn't. "We were told that Nelson wanted a divorce and Connie refused to give him one."

Ms. Tan's lips puckered like she'd downed a gulp that had too much lemon and not enough sugar. "Connie would have told me. Nelson was the most committed to working things out. More than Connie, even."

Jay shifted in his seat. Even though he'd decided to play a mute since we got here, at least that showed he knew that response wasn't any better for us. A husband who wanted out of a relationship might kill his wife. A husband whose wife wanted out and felt betrayed had an equally strong motive. The prosecution could play either side depending on what more people said. Knowing there were witnesses out there who could support either stance meant I couldn't argue either without the prosecution being able to present their counter.

Why was it that I couldn't ever seem to find an easy case?

Then again, my dad would say that defending the guilty wasn't easier, but it was more straightforward. Defending someone "innocent" meant you had to walk a line where innocence and guilt blurred and you saw exactly how good people could get themselves into trouble.

In this situation, the tricky part was how to define commitment and what that looked like.

Connie and Nelson might have been equally committed, but Nelson was working harder at mending their relationship. I couldn't assume that I understood what Ms. Tan meant when she talked about commitment.

I'd simply have to come at what I wanted to know carefully since I didn't want to offend Ms. Tan and make her think that I didn't believe her. "Nelson did tell us they'd been separated a long time. No one could blame Connie if her commitment to their marriage was flagging."

"Flagging. I wouldn't put it quite that way." Ms. Tan closed both hands around her glass and pulled it closer toward her, almost like a transparent shield. "It's just that..." Her gaze shifted in the direction of Connie's house, and her eyelashes fluttered like pressure built behind them. "Connie seemed more distant with both of us lately. Nelson even came and asked me if she's said anything to me. I told him I thought she hadn't been feeling well, but..."

She shook her head as if she couldn't find the words to finish. I waited and prayed Jay wouldn't pick this moment to fill in the silence with nervous prattle. Ms. Tan looked down at her hands and didn't continue.

"But?" Jay prompted, his voice the exact right balance of gentle and encouraging.

I kept my gaze from slipping to him. Maybe I shouldn't have assumed he'd be as unsure when he spoke to a client. His timing was perfect. I'd been about to do the same thing myself.

"Something was bothering her. I could tell the same as he could, but she clearly didn't want to talk to either of us about it. I was worried she'd decided she couldn't do the separation thing any more. Then her priest started visiting her at home, too. It made me hope it might be a spiritual crisis or something happening at the church where she worked."

My arms felt like spiders scurried over them.

Her priest started visiting her at home.

All evidence pointed to Father Napier lying about Connie wanting a divorce. Ms. Tan had confirmed that Connie would have told her. Connie's reticence to share whatever was bothering her was an anomaly.

Father Napier had also told me that Connie wanting a divorce wasn't something said in confidence. That confirmed that, if Connie had wanted a divorce, her best friend would have known.

Father Napier had lied. He'd lied knowing we couldn't technically prove she hadn't said it. The prosecution could easily convince jurors that Connie would have shared something with Father Napier that she hadn't felt comfortable sharing with anyone else, even if she hadn't told it to him in confidence.

But priests didn't normally make house calls.

He might have had a personal reason for lying about Connie wanting a divorce—a reason like he was breaking his vow of celibacy and one of the Ten Commandments by having an affair with a member of his congregation. What other reason would there be for him to start visiting her at her home rather than speaking with her at the church as they'd done before?

Father Napier was a lot older than her, and from what I'd seen, not traditionally attractive. But it wouldn't be the first time a woman was swept away by a man fitting that description if she were already vulnerable. The laws against people in certain positions starting romantic relationships with those in their care were in place specifically for those reasons. Abusing power and beginning a relationship that might be less than equal became too easy when one person depended on the other for something like spiritual or medical care or counselling.

It figured I was going to end up proving true the stereotype that I hated. If I'd had to choose, I almost would have preferred for Nelson to be guilty and the priest to be innocent.

"Do you know the priest's name?" Jay asked.

Apparently, he'd loosened his tongue from whatever glue had held it before. It wasn't a bad question, though, just an unnecessary one since I'd already spoken to her priest. He didn't know that, of course. On the way here, I'd filled him in on the basics of the case, but not the particulars.

Ms. Tan shook her head. "He was tall. Young. Maybe even younger than Connie and me. Very handsome. If he wasn't a priest, I would have called him stylish."

My heart hit the bottom of my throat hard enough to make me choke on the sip of lemonade I'd just taken.

That description didn't fit Father Napier.

It fit the priest I'd talked to when I first entered Holy Cross Catholic Church.

I couldn't get control of the coughing enough to ask a follow-up.

Jay jumped to his feet. His patio chair wobbled like it might fall over. "Do you need the Heimlich? I'm trained."

I waved for him to sit back down. If he knew the Heimlich well enough to perform it safely on a pregnant woman, he should have also known he couldn't Heimlich out a liquid. A liquid couldn't even get lodged in my throat.

My coughing continued long enough that even Ms. Tan shot me a concerned look.

"I think a bit got into my lungs," I managed to gasp out. "I'm fine."

I wasn't fine, though. Father Napier wasn't the priest who visited Connie, but that made it worse. Now it sounded like Father Napier lied to cover up something he knew the other priest had done. Instead of having one lying, sinning priest to deal with, I had two.

9

*I*nstead of having Jay take me home, I caught a ride back to White Cloud to Holy Cross Catholic Church. I needed to find out the name of the other priest and send it to Hal's private investigation firm and see if anything popped up. Even though Hal was away, his employees were still there and working.

If the other priest had been a priest long, this might not be the first time he broke his vows. Knowing his history would help us build an alternative explanation for what happened to Connie.

On the way there, I texted to Mark to ask if he could pick me up at the church after he finished the reports he'd gone into the office to work on.

Jay stopped right in front of the sidewalk that led up to the church's front doors rather than parking farther away to let me out. "Are you sure you don't want me to go with you, Mrs. Fitzhenry-Dawes?"

He really needed to stop calling me *Mrs.* Fitzhenry-Dawes. Not even my mom was Mrs. Fitzhenry-Dawes. "I appreciate you giving up so much of your day already."

I pulled at the door handle, but the door refused to budge. Jay hadn't put the car into park, releasing the automatic lock.

For once, my PTSD didn't flare up and presume some nefarious motive. Whether that spoke to progress on my part or Jay's character, I wasn't sure.

Instead, I turned back to him and lifted my eyebrows. Hopefully our baby would get Mark's expressive eyebrows instead of mine that would only rise as a pair.

Jay stared straight ahead, his hands gripping the steering wheel. "I know that I sent us to the wrong house, and that I didn't speak enough during the witness interview today. I just thought that she'd open up better to another woman rather than if it seemed like we were ganging up on her. Mr. Taylor made it clear to me that I could be dismissed during the three-month probationary period for any reason."

In some ways, Anderson modeled our business too much on my parents. They were known for putting the fear into new lawyers when they hired them because they wanted to see how they performed under pressure. "I'm not going to fire you."

"I hope you'll give me another chance to prove myself," he continued as if he hadn't heard me. "I'm willing to learn. I took this job because I want to learn from you."

His words petered out as I was considering whether I'd need to stop him.

Reassurances that I wasn't going to fire him jumped to my lips, but something in the way he'd phrased his last sentence made me pause. When he'd said *learn from you*, the *you* hadn't sounded plural. It'd sounded almost like he meant me specifically. I definitely didn't want to assume, though, and come off sounding like I was full of myself.

I shifted to face him better, even though the confines of the car and my huge belly made me feel like I was trying to wriggle into a wet suit. "First thing to learn is that you really need to call me Nicole. You'll be doing me a favor."

A wobbly smile crossed Jay's face as if he wasn't even sure if he was supposed to smile or not. I'd thought I lacked in self-confidence, but he might be even worse than I was.

"The second thing is that Anderson sounds a lot scarier than he is. He'll take the time when he gets back to teach you how he likes things done. No one will be firing you while you learn."

Jay tightened his tie. He still didn't make eye contact. "I want to learn from Mr. Taylor for sure, but I wanted to make a better impression on you than I feel like I made today. I heard you defend Clement Dodd and followed your cases after that. You catch things in cases that other people miss. I want to know how you do it."

Oh, that my dad could see this. He and I had come a long way in our relationship and our mutual respect, but he might not believe me if I told him that someone admired the way I practiced law. My secret wasn't much of a secret.

In fact, I'd been so focused on my own qualms over working a case with a potentially corrupt priest and on Jay's nervous demeanor that I hadn't paid attention to Ms. Tan the way I should have. Had Jay not asked for more information, I'd have jumped to conclusions that were wrong.

"No one's perfect." I smiled. Even though he wasn't looking at me, he should be able to hear it in my voice. "I listen to people, I watch them, and I try to see them as people rather than as suspects or criminals or witnesses I can use. Based on what I saw today, you have the instincts to do that, too. You read Ms. Tan well enough to know the perfect timing for asking the questions we needed asked."

His gaze swung to mine with a look that unabashedly said *really?*

"Even once I go on maternity leave, I can help you learn if you're willing to put in some out-of-work hours to watch old interview tapes."

Jay bobbed his head. "I can do that." He frowned slightly. "But if you weren't disappointed with my work today, why are you sending me home?"

So that's what had set this off. "I don't want you to have to drive another round trip, and I'll use the time to pray while I wait for my husband."

Jay's expression said he wasn't sure prayer would be time well spent, but he didn't say anything other than that he'd see me on Monday if I came into the office.

He put the car into park, and I climbed out.

Today the sign in front of the church read *Don't give up. Moses was once a basket case.*

Along with the continued sense of humor from whoever changed the sign each week, they'd also updated the newest blood drive date. It was too bad the names of the priests weren't listed as well the way my pastor's name was on our church's sign. If they had been, I could have done a quick search on the Internet to see if any pictures turned up. Ideally, I didn't want to arouse any suspicion by going around and asking the names of the priests who served there.

I pulled out my phone and checked the church's website just in case. Only Father Napier's name was listed. Presumably he was the senior priest.

Maybe inside there would be a list of the priests and nuns who worked here or a schedule for who was running certain programs or taking confessions. Aside from the fact that priests had to keep what they were told confidential, I didn't know any of the rules or norms surrounding confession.

If I were going to regular confession, though, I'd want to talk to the same priest every time. It seemed to make sense that people would feel more comfortable about being completely honest if they knew they could confide in a single priest rather than meeting with a new one each visit.

I slipped into the back of the church. More people sat in the pews than the weekday when I'd come before, and a woman even stood in front of the tiers of tea light candles, lighting one, her back to me. No priests were nearby, however.

I tiptoed along the line of pews toward the confessional. That seemed to be the most likely place where I'd find a list if there was one. Hopefully the people waiting their turn didn't think I was butting in line.

A frame holding a white piece of paper hung on the wall next to the confessional. From the edge of the pews, I couldn't tell what it was, but the odds seemed to be in my favor. Maybe they hung it on the door of the confessional when it wasn't staffed to let people know when they should come back. I headed toward it.

I took out my phone so I could snap a picture of the names if I was right, trying to look like just another parishioner, albeit one with a bad memory.

The door to the confessional swung open, almost cracking me in the belly. My shirt swished in the breeze from it, and I took an instinctive step back.

A man barged out of the confessional. He had broad shoulders like he might have played football in high school, but a waistline that said he hadn't played any sports recently. His expression was tight, like he'd been given a penance he didn't want to do.

He glanced at the phone in my hand. "Were you trying to record my confession?"

His voice came out rough and low. In any other place, no one but me would have been able to hear him, but the unnatural quiet of the sanctuary made it sound like he bellowed the words.

I looked at my phone without intending to. Someone loitering around the confessional with their phone out and on the screen that could be used to take video as easily as it could be used to snap a photo could look suspicious. I couldn't even hold it up and show him that it was on some innocent screen.

"I was going to take a picture of the confessional times so I could remember them." Even as I said it, it sounded like a lie. People didn't take pictures of times and dates. They put them in their calendar.

And it was a lie. It just wasn't the lie he would assume it was.

He took a step forward. "There should be a penalty for people who snoop on confession."

I took another step back. My rational brain knew he wasn't actually threatening to hurt me, a pregnant woman, standing in a church in front of a dozen or more witnesses. If I had actually been trying to record his conversation with the priest, he'd be justifiably angry. I'd be angry if I was Catholic and confessing and someone had not only been trying to listen in on what I was saying in confidence but was also attempting to make a record of it that could be shared.

My rational brain knew all that, but my body didn't.

Blood rushed into my head. Or maybe it was away from it. The room seemed to wobble like a Californian earthquake was happening in Michigan.

I stumbled slightly and dropped my purse. Everything in it

spilled out over the floor. Black dots flickered at the edges of my vision, and my skin felt sticky and hot.

An arm slid around me and helped me backward until I sat in a pew. I couldn't exactly put my head between my knees. I couldn't see my knees.

"Are you alright?" a different man's voice asked. It sounded vaguely familiar, but I couldn't place it. My vision was too spotty to see him clearly, but he knelt in front of me.

I nodded. "Just dizzy. Thanks to the baby."

"Breathe slowly and deeply." He stood to his feet. "There are penalties, Mr. Bird, and not only for priests. Any Catholic who accidentally overhears the sacrament of confession and breaks it can be excommunicated."

"What if she's not Catholic?" The position of Mr. Bird's voice had moved. He wasn't above me anymore, despite my seated position. He seemed to be closer to the floor.

I sucked in air even though I was sure hyperventilation hadn't caused my dizzy spell. Sitting seemed to be helping, though. My vision cleared slightly.

Mr. Bird was down on the floor, picking up the contents of my purse in all its embarrassing glory of old receipts, at least two Chapsticks, tissues, and more pens than I could count. The business card holder my parents had given me last Christmas had also fallen out and popped open, my cards everywhere.

Mr. Bird had a few of them in his hands, but he was glaring at me.

Yup, those most certainly made it look like I was lying about what I'd been doing. He'd probably been in there confessing about some affair or shady business deal and thought I was a lawyer hired by someone with an interest in his dealings to get proof of the sordid details.

He'd figure out eventually that I was telling the truth when he never saw me again.

"I don't think she'd be here if she wasn't Catholic," the other man said.

I shifted my gaze to him, and my visions tilted slightly again.

It was the younger priest who fit the description of the priest who'd been "making house calls" to Connie Burke.

If he did have something to do with Connie's death and he spotted my business cards, he might not be so sure of my innocence. Worse, he'd know I was looking into him and his relationship with her.

10

*B*efore I could think of what to do, Mr. Bird held out one of my business cards to the priest. "She's a lawyer."

The priest took it, but then he knelt down next to Mr. Bird, scooped up the remainder of the cards, and placed them all back inside the holder. "Lawyers can have faith, too. In fact, many of them need confession and penance the most."

His voice carried a hint of teasing. It could have been directed at Mr. Bird, or it could have been directed at me. As much as I wanted to defend my chosen profession, he was probably right. Still, if he'd meant it to mock me, it hardly seemed fitting for a priest.

Then again, I suspected the same priest of potentially sleeping with a married woman and murdering her, so poking fun at someone he'd just met was the lesser offense.

And my secret identity was out in the open. The priest might not suspect me of anything relating to Connie Burke's murder immediately, but he'd no doubt hear soon enough that I was defending Nelson. When that happened, his guard would be up and my job would be harder.

Whatever the priest had intended by his statement about lawyers, Mr. Bird nodded grudgingly and took the business card case from him. He shoved it back into my purse with the other things he'd already collected.

He climbed to his feet. "I'm sorry for losing my temper."

He pronounced it *sore-y* rather than *sari*. Coming from the melting pot of Washington, DC, I'd learn to recognize a lot of regional accents. I wasn't sure where this one marked him as originating from, but he wasn't from Michigan.

He handed my purse to me. "If you were close enough to hear anything, you'd know my temper's why I need to come to confession so often."

He gave me a small smile that said *truce?* His expression looked like he was waiting to gauge my reaction.

"I think you should add anger management classes to the penance we already talked about." The priest set a hand on Mr. Bird's arm. "Understood?"

Something flickered across Mr. Bird's face that seemed closer to fear than to more anger, but he simply nodded and walked away.

Something was definitely not right with this priest. Parishioners shouldn't be frightened of the people who were supposed to be caring for their spiritual needs.

Though it was possible I'd read everything wrong. My head did still feel like it was filled with helium and trying to float away.

The young priest turned back to me. "I hope you can accept Mr. Bird's apology. His wife died recently. Grief and guilt are complicated things."

That much I knew from personal experience. Everyone reacted to grief differently. Some people blamed others. Some people blamed themselves for what they'd lost. Some people blamed the person they'd lost. If there was anything grief wasn't, it was straightforward and easy to understand.

"Now," he knelt down again next to me, "I don't think you should be driving yourself home. Is there someone you can call to pick you up?"

I'd already planned to call Mark to pick me up, but before I called anyone, I needed to know this priest's name. Otherwise, this whole stressful run-in would be a waste of time.

"I'm okay, Father..." I let my sentence drag so he'd fill in the gap and tried not to think about the fact that he'd mostly likely think I was fishing for his name because of how handsome he was. He was probably flirted with all the time, even by married, very pregnant women.

A hand brushed softly against my shoulder, and I jerked.

"She's a friend of mine, Father," Vivienne McTavish's voice said from above and behind me. "I can drive her home, and I'll make sure she's okay so we don't keep you any longer from hearing confessions."

What was Vivienne doing here? I glanced back over my shoulder. It was definitely her. She wore the same coat as the woman I'd spotted lighting a candle when I came in. I hadn't recognized her from behind.

And she didn't look happy to see me.

The priest glanced at the people who sat still waiting and gave her a smile. "Thank you."

Vivienne stood quietly behind me while the priest went back into the confessional, and another person took the side that Mr. Bird had vacated.

I slid my legs into the pew so I was sitting on the bench properly rather than being perched on the end. Vivienne sat next to me.

"Were you actually dizzy?" Her voice was low enough that no one else would hear us. "Or was that a ploy to find a way to speak with the Father about Connie Burke's murder?"

Ouch. Harsh. Also kind of fair. I hadn't thought about faking a dizzy spell, but it was the kind of thing I might have done if it would have benefited my investigation. Vivienne knew me well enough from Chief McTavish's stories about me that she knew it, too. The couple of times we'd gotten together socially wouldn't have wiped away my track record.

"Real dizzy spell. The baby is pressing on a nerve that it shouldn't be." Turnabout was fair play, though. I wasn't the only one here who shouldn't have been. There was a Catholic church in Fair Haven. Connie Burke attended in White Cloud instead because she worked here, but if Vivienne were Catholic, why hadn't she attended closer to home? "Are you here about the case?"

Vivienne gave me a look that reminded me a lot of Chief McTavish when I'd done something particularly off-the-wall in pursuit of the truth. I suddenly wasn't sure whether she'd picked up the look from him or him from her. It seemed so natural on Vivienne's face. Maybe twenty-five years from now Mark and I would share expressions.

"This is my church," Vivienne said. "I'm here for the reasons people go to their church."

Heat burned the back of my neck like I'd fallen asleep out in the sun. I hadn't meant it how it'd sounded. It could have easily sounded like I thought she was too smart or modern a woman to believe in God. That wasn't it at all.

Believing in God—in my opinion, anyway—was the smart, logical choice. "I didn't mean...what I meant..."

Everything I tried to come up with to explain sounded worse than what I'd already said.

"It's okay, Nicole." She sighed softly, sounding like her husband again. "What you wanted to know is why I'm not attending a church closer to home, right?"

I nodded.

"It always seemed safer to pick a church outside of whatever town Owen had been sent to. That way I wasn't as likely to meet someone who might be involved in his investigation. When we came to Fair Haven, I didn't realize we'd stay this time. By the time I did, I didn't want to switch churches again."

All I could come up with in response to that was, "Oh."

I knew better than probably anyone other than Chief McTavish how much she was struggling to fit in back in Fair Haven. The people weren't ostracizing her the way they had me, but she'd spent so many years moving from place to place and not knowing who they could trust because Chief McTavish had been assigned to investigate internal corruption. Those habits of keeping herself separate would be tough to break.

Vivienne stood to her feet. "Do you need a hand, or are you steadier now?"

My body felt like it was solid rather than liquid again. "I'm okay."

"Time to head home, then."

I followed her out of the church.

I hadn't gotten the name of the priest that I'd come for, but Vivienne clearly knew him. Asking her for his name would raise less suspicion anyway.

She pressed her clicker, and a nearby car beeped. I waited until we'd both climbed in.

"What's the name of the priest who helped me when I was dizzy?" I was about to give her the excuse that I'd like to send him a thank-you note, but she was Chief McTavish's wife. Even though she wasn't a law enforcement officer herself, she'd see through any excuse I made for wanting his name.

Vivienne pulled out of the parking space without so much as looking my way. "I know what you're doing. He didn't have anything to do with Connie's death. No one here did. She was well-liked."

That objection was one I would have expected from almost anyone else. But it was surprisingly naïve from Vivienne, who knew as well as anyone how well evil could hide, and that even well-liked people could be murdered. Moreover, that well-liked people could be murderers.

It also made sense. She hadn't had a permanent home, or a permanent church home, in a long time. Now that she'd found one, she wanted to defend it and the people within it.

But whether she liked it or not, one of the church members had been murdered.

The memory of the priest's apology for Mr. Bird flashed into my mind. One woman had been murdered, and another had died. For all I knew, Mrs. Bird's death had been a long time ago. But if that were the case, then the priest would have been less likely to give it as an excuse.

"The man I upset today—was his wife's death suspicious, too?"

Vivienne signaled and pulled into the parking lot of a small café. "If we're going to do this, we might as well do it over coffee. This is where Owen and I come after church when he's able to attend with me."

In some ways, she was a woman after my own heart. Thankfully, I hadn't had a coffee yet today.

The café smelled like freshly ground coffee beans and warm chocolate. My mouth watered. Maybe I'd have a hot chocolate instead.

If this was a diversion tactic by Vivienne, it might be working. With the aromas around me, I could barely keep my mind on the case.

I ordered not only a hot chocolate, but a big slice of lemon loaf, too. After all, I needed to feed the baby.

Vivienne picked a table for us in a corner. It looked out on the street. The view wasn't anything memorable, but it made sense as a spot a police officer would want to sit. He'd have his back to a wall and a view of both the street and the rest of the café. No one could sneak up on them or eavesdrop without him spotting them. Vivienne took the chair that would put her back to the room.

This was likely the table she and Chief McTavish always chose if it was open. She sat in the chair he wouldn't want by habit.

She swirled her coffee around in its cup as if instinctively knowing it would be too hot. "I haven't been a police officer's wife for years for nothing. When Connie was killed"—she didn't even flinch over the word the way most people would, especially if they'd known the deceased—"I had Owen look for a connection between her death and Lauren Bird's."

The fact that she'd already had Chief McTavish check and yet still insisted to me that the members and leaders of her church were innocent told me what she'd found.

"Other than that they technically both attended Holy Cross Catholic Church, there's no connection between them," Vivienne said.

Not that I was doubting Chief McTavish's skills. He was one of the best police officers I'd ever met, even including those my parents went head-to-head with in DC. But I wasn't going to drop my investigation on the basis of *I promise that the two deaths have nothing in common and that no one here was involved.* Not even from Vivienne. I might not have even let it go at that from Mark.

I'd been tricked by seemingly unrelated deaths before. "How were they different?"

Vivienne didn't sigh, but she looked like she wanted to. She also looked like she'd expected me to want details, which was why she'd brought us here where we could at least do it in comfort, with snacks.

"Connie's death was a murder. Lauren's was probably a suicide."

An inconclusive suicide could be a murder, but a suicide fit better with what the younger priest had let drop about Mr. Bird feeling guilt and grief.

I broke off a chunk of the lemon loaf and chewed slowly since my coffee was also still too hot. I met Vivienne's gaze to let her know I was waiting for more.

She shook her head but smiled a little. "Even that they both attended our church is a stretch. Connie was faithful. She attended everything. She baked for the bake sales even though she was allergic to eggs and couldn't eat most of it. She volunteered at the blood drives and donated blood whenever she was able even though she fainted every time. If she could be at the church, she was." She took the tiniest sip of her coffee and grimaced, rolling her lips like she'd burnt her tongue. "Lauren's husband started coming shortly before her death, but only to confession. I don't remember if Lauren ever came herself."

I stuffed more lemon loaf into my mouth so I didn't have to

respond immediately. Vivienne hadn't been kidding. Even the connection with the church hadn't been more than passing. The most they seemed to have in common was that they were both woman and both married.

While it wasn't outside of the realm of possibility that their husbands knew each other and that was the connection, it seemed unlikely. Chief McTavish was too good an investigator to overlook any link or lead, especially when it came as a request from his wife. While he'd never directly said so, I'd gotten the impression that he regretted dragging her from place to place in the pursuit of his career and the stress and isolation the constant moves had caused her.

Though it seemed like she was making up for it now with getting involved in a church community. They'd been living in Fair Haven for less than a year and a half, and they'd decided to stay in Fair Haven permanently less than a year ago.

Considering I'd come close to insulting her more than once today, I ought to extend an olive branch now. "You seem to know a lot about the people there."

She shrugged. "I've been trying to get to know people now that we've settled in one place."

Once again, I saw the woman I'd seen the first day I met her. The one who didn't unpack her boxes anymore if she didn't think she was going to be in one place long enough to use what was in them. The one who had acquaintances, but no friends.

"How are you finding it?"

She looked down at her coffee. "I'm having a much easier time learning about other people than letting other people learn about me, if I'm being honest."

I'd seen that, too. She watched a lot. She asked questions. She rarely ever volunteered any information about herself.

The fact that I'd had coffee with her a few times, had eaten dinner at her house, and had invited her and Chief McTavish to the Movies in the Woods we hosted at Sugarwood this summer and yet I didn't know she was a Catholic only drove it home.

And maybe that was my fault. I hadn't wanted her to feel like I was a pushy lawyer, using my skills to manipulate her into sharing with me. I'd wanted to be her friend, so I'd been waiting for her to feel comfortable opening up.

Maybe she needed more time. Or maybe I needed a different approach. Vivienne was a hard woman for even me to read. She'd had to learn to be that way, but I could see how it would hurt her chances for normal friendships.

The benefit of that came in how much she was able to observe because she wanted to learn about other people more than she wanted to share about herself.

And as an observant woman and a police chief's wife, the way to get her to help me with this might be to lay out the facts that I knew and see if she drew the same conclusions.

"I spoke to Connie's friend who lives next door. She thought Connie might be having a spiritual crisis. One of the priests, the priest who was taking confession today, was at her house a lot. At all hours."

Vivienne's lips moved slightly, as if she were going to say something. She didn't. Instead she ran her finger along the handle of her mug. Her gaze shifted away from me and onto a wall, then moved slowly back.

"I see," she said.

Mark sometimes said the same words when he didn't know how

to respond to a statement I'd made. In Vivienne's case, though, they sounded different, like they meant something different. They didn't sound like she was acknowledging that she'd heard me and needed time to process.

The words from her sounded more like she'd figured something out.

Something about the way she said it, the tone, also made me think that what she'd figured out and what I assumed weren't the same thing. Her tone said *I get it now* as if she'd figured out a puzzle. It didn't say *I've been betrayed* as if she'd been lied to.

Unfortunately, I obviously didn't see what she saw.

She tapped a short fingernail on the mug handle. "I know what you must have assumed when you heard that. It's not what you think. I'm pretty sure I know what was actually going on, and it might still be related to your case."

ivienne's voice and Father Jesse's voice alternated back and forth behind the closed door of his office. I caught a word here and there. Lawyer. Confidentiality. Catholic. Please.

Sitting out here, letting Vivienne show my hand to a suspect without me even being in the room to see his reaction, felt wrong on every level. But I had to trust her. She knew the importance of reading reactions and all the other reasons I wouldn't have wanted to tip Father Jesse off to my suspicions of him, but she still insisted on doing it this way.

The door to his office opened. "Please come in, Mrs. Cavanaugh."

I hoisted myself to my feet. The baby felt like it'd shifted around today somehow, even since this morning. My hips ached from the pressure, and I felt like I waddled more than walked. I both wished the baby was already here and was glad I had a few more days before he or she was.

Father Jesse—thinking about a priest by his first name still seemed wrong, but that's how Vivienne introduced him—motioned to the chair next to where Vivienne sat.

"You've forced me to lead one of my congregation astray," Father Jesse said in a way that might have been teasing but also might not have been.

He seemed to have one of those senses of humor where you could never quite tell if they were serious or not, and if they weren't serious, whether they were laughing at you or good-naturedly ribbing you.

"Not intentionally." I took the offered seat. At this point, my body ached so much all over that I didn't care what my dad would say about properly placing myself to control the interview. We'd lost that advantage anyway with the way Vivienne had insisted on doing this. "I wasn't recording whatever he was saying in the confessional. I wasn't here for him at all."

"Nor are you Catholic."

Guilty on that one. "I am a Christian."

He went around his desk and sank into his own chair. For a second, he looked a little less polished, a little less trained, and a little more like a man who had faced more stress than any person should have to bear lately. It was strange to see the human being behind the clerical robes. Watching a minister of any denomination on Sunday mornings made it easy to feel like they must be perfect.

"You've created a problem, though," he said. "The penalty for breaking the sanctity of confession is excommunication. Excommunication means nothing to you. Vee has vouched for you, but I know how lawyers are. You'll promise anything so long as you get the information you need to win your case."

Now that was downright insulting.

My parents were proof that it was also accurate at times. They would have had no trouble wringing information from a priest and then using it however they needed to.

I'd fought for a long time to prove I wasn't like my parents. Apparently, I'd have to re-fight this fight with every new person I met. "As a lawyer, I understand confidentiality. But if anything Connie Burke said to you can help solve her murder, doesn't it seem like the greater good is to share that, at least in a way that won't violate your vows?"

His look said *touché*. "That's what Vivienne has been arguing. She tells me that your heart is right, and that you won't give up on this path until you know for sure that I didn't play a part in Connie's death."

Vivienne had made an argument that he couldn't ignore if he was innocent. Anyone who had cared for Connie and wasn't involved in her death would want to make sure the investigation headed in the right direction.

"I don't think what you know dishonors Connie's memory," Vivienne said softly from beside me. "I disagreed with her. But it didn't diminish my respect for her."

Father Jesse touched a hand to his stiff, white clerical collar as if he desperately wanted to loosen it. He nodded his head.

Then he said nothing. It was like he'd taken an Unbreakable Vow from Harry Potter and was still subconsciously afraid of the consequences if he spoke.

Vivienne must have read assent in his nod, though. She turned toward me. "Father Jesse came to me a little over a month ago to ask about a hypothetical situation."

Which she must have known immediately meant the situation wasn't hypothetical at all. Did anyone actually ask about truly hypothetical situations, or was that word used entirely to cover bases?

My parents had often used it when they wanted to try to build the foundation for a plea deal without giving anything away. Hypothetically, if we knew this and told you that, what would you offer us?

But I couldn't imagine what kind of hypothetical situation Father Jesse would have needed to ask Vivienne about. If he'd been having an affair with Connie, he would be approaching his superior with a hypothetical, not a member of his congregation.

Vivienne had turned back to Father Jesse as if she expected she'd broken the ice enough.

"I knew Vivienne was married to a police officer." He actually gave a little tug on his collar this time. "I thought she'd either know what the punishment for a crime was or she could find out."

No wonder he was giving off nervous tells. Since he'd been asking about a hypothetical situation, it didn't technically violate confidentiality, but it came about as close as one could get. Some might argue it crossed the line in the same way that flirting could be considered unfaithfulness depending on how you looked at it.

More importantly for me was the motivation behind it all. He must not have been asking legal advice for himself. He'd have gone to a lawyer for that. Plus, Vivienne mentioned dishonoring Connie's memory.

So this was about something Connie had done. He must have gone to Vivienne because he knew she was a Catholic, and he trusted her to keep whatever he asked her to himself.

That spoke to Vivienne's character. Perhaps it wasn't just that she was a Catholic. Perhaps it was that she was both a Catholic and a police chief's wife. She knew how to keep a secret.

All the flippancy that I'd noticed in Father Jesse before was missing now. His throat worked, but no more words came out.

"What was the crime?" I asked.

I tried to keep my tone neutral. I couldn't sound too compassionate or he might see me as a person rather than a lawyer and be worried about confidentiality again. I couldn't sound too professional or he might go back to thinking I would do whatever it took —including lie—to free Nelson.

Father Jesse sucked in a breath. "Kidnapping."

I sucked in a breath, too. I couldn't help it. That wasn't what I'd been expecting.

Who had Connie planned to...oh.

The memory of the little boy eating cookies straight from the box jumped into my mind. His mother had thought we were from social services, and she'd said something snarky about Connie.

"Her next-door neighbor's son," I said.

It all made sense now. Connie, the woman who wasn't able to have children of her own, couldn't stand to see a little boy neglected —maybe even abused—by his mother. The neighbor had thought we were *more* social service workers. That meant some had already come, and yet her son was still with her.

Father Jesse shot me a look that made me think he wished being ordained a priest brought with it telepathic powers. "You knew?"

I shook my head. "I put the pieces together just now. I accidentally went to the wrong house when I was trying to talk to Connie's friend."

He leaned against his desk, then straightened up as if he remembered he wasn't supposed to show weakness in public. He was supposed to be dignified. A leader. "Connie was waiting for me one day when I finished confession. She asked me what she should do if she learned about something wrong that another person had done. It was all vague at first. The more upset she got about what was happening, the more specific details she gave me. Then she came to me with her plan."

My legs shook slightly. Thankfully I was already seated. What kind of position did that put him in? Not only with Connie, but with other people who might confess crimes to him that they'd committed. Or wanted to commit.

As a lawyer, I had that one protection. I had a duty to report any ongoing or future criminal activity if I knew my client was going to commit it. Lawyer–client privilege only covered crimes committed in the past.

From what I'd read about the sanctity of the confessional, priests didn't have that out. They had to keep everything quiet. If someone came to them and confessed that they were engaged in drug trafficking, there wasn't anything the priest could do except tell them that they needed to forego their criminal activities. If they came to them to tell them they were fantasizing about or even planning to kidnap someone, murder someone, or steal something, a priest could only plead with them not to go through with it.

If there was anything a priest had to report, it'd be a very short list.

On one level, it made sense. For anyone to confess their evil thoughts with honesty, they needed to know that nothing they said would leave the confessional. On another level, I knew it had to be one of the biggest challenges a priest faced.

I couldn't do it. I hadn't done it. Which was why I was under probation.

"I tried to talk her out of it," he said. "I helped her make the report to social services. It didn't seem to change much. She was desperate. I even slept on her couch the nights she knew her neighbor would be leaving her son by himself. She wasn't sure she could withstand the temptation."

That explained why Ms. Tan saw him there more often than was appropriate for a normal priest–parishioner relationship. The situation would have looked like an illicit affair or a dire spiritual crisis to anyone from the outside.

It'd turned out it was a spiritual crisis. Father Jesse wanted to stop Connie from committing a crime. He wanted to help her find a legal way to help a neglected child.

And I'd assumed the worst of him. I'd become the TV cliché that I despised. I should have had more trust in someone who claimed to be a man of God.

"Did she have the beginning of a plan to kidnap the little boy?" I asked, more because I wanted to keep him talking than because it mattered.

"Pieces of it. She'd found a guy who said he could make her a fake passport for the boy. She hadn't figured out where to go or how she'd get a job in another country. But she thought about it enough that I tried to be there as much as I could."

Sort of like he might have done with an alcoholic who wanted to break the habit and was in danger of a relapse.

Father Jesse couldn't have been with her every moment that she wasn't at work. He'd gone over whenever they knew Connie's neighbor would be leaving her son alone.

What about a time when her neighbor left at an irregular time?

Connie might have been too tempted. She might have gone over to try to take him, even without a fully formed plan. All she'd have needed to do was start driving. The Canadian border wasn't far away. If she already had a fake passport ready, she could have been across the border within a few hours. From there, she could have taken a flight to anywhere.

And if her neighbor came back and caught Connie trying to kidnap her son, it could have resulted in a fight that got out of hand. The mother might have been drunk and stabbed Connie. Or she simply might have bided her time and planned Connie's murder.

Stopping Connie from kidnapping her child spoke to motive. It also left a lot of gaps. Would Connie's neighbor have known enough about Nelson to be able to drive to his house and plant the blood? How would she have found out Nelson's address? Plus, she would have needed to collect enough of Connie's blood to plant on Nelson.

It also didn't explain why Father Napier lied about Nelson wanting a divorce. Maybe he'd been mistaken. Priests spoke to a lot of people and heard a lot of confessions. No doubt keeping them all straight sometimes became a challenge.

All the gaps didn't give me enough to form a solid defense for Nelson. Yet. It did give me a new place to start looking.

12

*V*ivienne walked with me back outside. She was still my ride home, after all. I'd already texted Mark not to come pick me up.

"I can vouch for Father Jesse's story. He asked me about Connie's situation long before her murder." Vivienne's voice dipped. "I didn't know he was talking about her until you told me you thought they were having an affair. Bits and pieces started to make sense then."

I nodded absently. That's often how it worked. So much of my job was a matter of paying attention to all the details and hoping my brain would make connections between them.

Right now, I needed more details. The next step seemed to be to go back to Connie's neighborhood and talk to her other neighbor.

Just not today. My body begged me to take a nap. I didn't know what it would be like to care for our baby outside my body, but it had to be less physically draining than carrying it inside, didn't it?

Besides, Vivienne had likely been planning to go home hours ago. "Thanks for your help today and for the ride."

She nodded.

I felt like I should say something more, try to reach out to her in some way. I'd spent most of the time with her essentially accusing her spiritual leader of breaking a full third of the Ten Commandments.

Then again, she was Chief McTavish's wife. Police officers didn't apologize for digging and pushing and accusing. They had to do it. It was their job. Finding the truth and protecting innocent people often depended on it.

My job was similar. If anyone would understand that and not need an explanation or apology, Vivienne was probably the one.

"When are you planning to interview Connie's neighbor?" Vivienne asked.

Not *are you* but *when*. She knew my next steps almost as well as I did. I just wouldn't have called it interviewing. That sounded too much like I was with the police.

When I could go depended on who I could get to drive me. Mandy was off the table, as was Russ. Russ would willingly drive me to medical appointments, but he wouldn't take me to talk to a potential suspect. At least not without coming inside with me and glaring at the woman the whole time. That would be worse than Mandy coming inside and being too obvious about why we were there.

I could ask Jay again. After our conversation today, he'd happily go with me, but it wouldn't be the greatest learning experience for him. I wanted to have a driver and "backup" in the car, but my instincts said I'd get more out of Connie's neighbor if I spoke to her alone. She seemed to have issues with authority. Two people coming to speak with her together immediately seemed like we were putting ourselves in a superior position. People in positions of authority almost always came in twos to situations where they anticipated problems. The subconscious cues would put her on edge if I took someone in with me.

None of that musing answered Vivienne's question. "I'll need to wait for Mark to take me. My dizzy spells mean I can't drive myself."

She made an *mmm* sound, as if to indicate that I'd explained the whole near fainting episode from earlier to her satisfaction. She finally believed me that I hadn't faked it.

The fact that she'd still had doubts said something about me. Whether that something was good or bad depended on your perspective. My parents would say good.

"I could drive you." Vivienne's voice was firm but soft. "Other than my church activities, I don't have much to do with my time."

AFTER VIVIENNE DROPPED ME OFF, I SAT ON MY COUCH AND TURNED my phone end over end. I'd typed in the direct number for Chief McTavish's work line, but I hadn't yet pressed the button to dial.

Vivienne was so sure that Father Jesse hadn't had anything to do with Connie's death, but Father Napier had still lied. He'd said that Nelson wanted a divorce, and Connie refused to give him one. Everyone else who knew them said otherwise.

He might have mixed Connie and Nelson up with another couple. With so many people's spiritual needs to care for, a mix-up wasn't out of the realm of possibility.

Still, if it wasn't a mix-up, why had he done it? And just because Father Jesse had been helping prevent a kidnapping, did that mean he couldn't possibly have killed her?

I turned the phone over again to stare at the number. Calling

Chief McTavish to ask if he'd checked the alibis of both priests seemed disloyal to Vivienne somehow.

Friendships don't belong in the courtroom, my dad always said.

He regularly played golf with one of DC's chief prosecutors, but once they stepped into the courtroom on opposite sides, you wouldn't have known it. In fact, their friendship outside the courtroom often made them fiercer and meaner inside it.

If Vivienne ever found out, hopefully she would understand that I couldn't simply take her words for things because she was my friend. This wasn't a situation where she was telling me that *she* hadn't committed a crime. I would have believed her then. In this case, she might have been deceived.

Besides, she was a police officer's wife. She had to understand the value of evidence.

I tapped my screen, and the call went through.

"McTavish," the gruff voice said from the other end.

Pots clanged in the background. I glanced at my screen. Crap. I'd dialed his work *cell* phone rather than his office number. From the background noise, he was at home with Vivienne.

"I need you to step away from where Vivienne is and not give away who's calling," I said softly, even though Vivienne wouldn't be able to hear my voice through the phone over the cooking noises.

McTavish sighed, but then I heard muffled words that sounded like "I need to take this in my office."

The sounds around him faded, and I heard a click like a door closing.

"You'd better have a good explanation for all the cloak and dagger, Dawes."

Never a good sign when McTavish went back to truncating my last name. "Neither of us wants to upset Vivienne."

The pause on his end stretched, and then was broken by the squeak of a desk chair. "Go ahead. But be quick. It's spaghetti and meatball night."

The image of Chief McTavish trying to eat spaghetti in a dignified manner made me smile. I squelched it so he wouldn't hear it in my voice. "I know that Vivienne is convinced that neither of the priests where Connie Burke worked were involved with her death, but did you check where they were at Connie's time of death?"

"I did check." His words came out slow, as if admitting it was admitting that he also felt guilty for circumventing his wife's judgment. "Because of when Mrs. Burke died, both men say they were asleep in their own rooms in the rectory. They saw each other over coffee and then headed to a staff meeting at the church together at eight am. The church secretary and three nuns confirmed it."

I flipped open the notepad where I'd written down the times for everything we knew for sure in the case. Mark had put the time of death for Connie Burke sometime around six-thirty am, based on her liver temperature. Nelson's apartment building didn't have any surveillance cameras, so we hadn't been able to prove when he returned to his apartment. He'd told me he thought it was around seven am, and he went right to sleep.

Connie hadn't attended the church staff meeting, which is what made the other staff members concerned enough to try to reach her. When they hadn't been able to reach her, they'd eventually called the police.

So we knew Connie was dead or dying by the time the staff meeting started.

"It's not conclusive," Chief McTavish said, "but..."

But that timeline meant that while neither of them had alibis for the time of Connie's death, they also wouldn't have had time to plant the blood on Nelson and make it to the staff meeting. Especially not if they needed to change their own blood-covered clothes first.

Vivienne had been right. Neither Father Napier nor Father Jesse had killed Connie Burke. Father Napier must have been mistaken about the divorce.

Connie's next-door neighbor looked more like the most likely culprit all the time.

TRUE TO HER WORD, VIVIENNE PICKED ME UP THE FOLLOWING week and drove me to Connie's neighborhood. I wanted to ask her if Chief McTavish knew she was helping me, but I decided that might make things awkward. If she hadn't told him, she was basically hiding things from her husband for me. If she had told him, I'd only want to pry more about how *that* conversation had gone.

She pulled up in front of the correct house without me having to tell her which side it was. Then again, it was the only house on the street that looked a bit like a mangy stray dog in among a pack of purebreds.

"Do you want to call my phone and leave it on in your pocket?" Vivienne asked as I unsnapped my seatbelt. "Owen said you attract more murderers than garbage does flies."

Well, overlooking that rather graphic description, at least I knew she'd told him. And it wasn't a terrible idea. Since we weren't recording the conversation, it also wasn't technically illegal. Not only would it give me more of a safety net than simply having her sit out here, but it would also give me a second set of ears. The advantage of working in teams was the ability to discuss what you'd discovered afterward.

As long as nothing I shared with her was considered confidential information from Nelson, we'd be fine.

I dialed her number, then turned the volume on my phone down to almost nothing. The last thing I needed was for a car to honk near Vivienne and have it be loud enough for Connie's neighbor to hear. That would make her suspicious and end the conversation.

Vivienne pulled a set of earbuds out of her purse and connected them to her phone, then she tucked her phone into a cup holder. Smart. She didn't want to put it on speaker because then it would pick up more ambient noise and transmit that to my phone, but she also didn't want to prop the phone up to her ear for however long the conversation took.

Too bad Chief McTavish couldn't have used her more in his own cases. She held a level of intelligence that most people probably didn't realize.

I put my own phone on speaker to help the sound carry. Instead of putting the phone back into my purse where the sound would be too muffled, I tucked it into my pocket. She'd have to turn her own sound way up, but she should be able to hear most of the conversation.

My first knock on the door went unanswered.

I knocked again.

The wooden door behind the screen door cracked open and a small face peeked out. "I'm not supposed to let anyone in when my mom's not home."

My heart felt like little cracks splintered across its surface. If I'd been dangerous, he'd have just told me that there was no one there to protect him. And he didn't know any better than to announce it. While I couldn't condone Connie wanting to break the law to rescue him, I couldn't condemn her, either. A voice in the back of my head told me to grab him up and run right now. If I'd been allowed to lift anything heavier than a glass of water, I might have.

"Do you know when your mom will be home?" I asked instead.

He looked past me. For a second, I thought he might not understand the question. Then I heard a car door slam.

His mother came up the walk toward us. A slight movement inside Vivienne's car told me she'd seen it all.

The woman stopped at the bottom of the steps. "Are you stupid or something?"

My mouth sagged slightly. *You're not a fish, Nicole,* my mom's voice reminded me. *You're a lawyer.*

I snapped my mouth shut, but all I could think to say was, "I'm sorry?"

"I'm still not Ms. Tan, and this still isn't her house."

Oh, right. I guess it would look a little strange for me to show up here again. "I came to talk to you this time."

The muscles around her eyes tensed, and she shifted the bag in her arms. It was a paper grocery bag, but the soft noise that came from inside sounded like liquid swishing and glass bottles clinking together.

Considering she'd left her young son alone to go out and buy alcohol, her suspicion might be warranted. Just because I'd come to speak to Ms. Tan last time didn't mean I wasn't secretly from social services. I could have been there asking Ms. Tan if she'd noticed anything concerning.

"My name's Nicole..." I started to say Fitzhenry-Dawes since I practiced under my maiden name, but it felt like the wrong play here. I was obviously—very obviously—pregnant. She'd assume that one last name was mine and one was my husband's. Some people had strange opinions of people with hyphenated last names. Like they were trying to set themselves apart and be different or more enlightened. Based on the little I'd seen of her, any hint of that would turn her against me. "Nicole Cavanaugh."

The look she gave me made it seem like she suspected I was lying. My pause had been a little too long. The only other explanation was that I'd forgotten my own last name.

"I'll thank you to get off my porch, Nicole *Cavanaugh*." She slurred my last name the way some people chose to sneer Fitzhenry-Dawes. "We don't need whatever product you're selling."

That was an assumption I wouldn't have jumped to. I'd been accused of being worse, though, so maybe I'd count that as a partial win.

"I'm a lawyer working the Connie Burke murder case." I'd learned that, if I didn't explicitly state that I was a defense attorney, people could jump to the conclusion that I was a prosecuting attorney. If this woman had killed Connie, I wanted her to think I was looking elsewhere. "I'm speaking to all her neighbors."

For a second, she looked like she was considering shouldering past me. "I'm not testifying in court."

Technically, she'd have to if she was subpoenaed. But quibbling about that didn't seem to be worth it. "All I need is for you to answer a few questions."

"If I do that, will you get off my porch?"

I almost said *cross my heart and hope to die*, but then I remembered that Vivienne was listening and she'd been warned by Chief McTavish about how many times I had nearly died in the pursuit of a case. Besides, it didn't seem very professional. "I'll leave as soon as I've asked my questions."

She jerked her head toward the door. "Then get out of my way. This is heavy."

The little boy pulled the wooden door open. The only place for me to go to get out of her way was forward into the house, so I tried the screen door. It wasn't locked. Had we been in DC, that would have surprised me. Here in Fair Haven, almost half of the residents didn't lock their doors.

Connie had been one of them, and look where that got her. Though even locking a door didn't guarantee anything. Nelson had locked his door and look what happened to him. Plus, there were ways around locks.

The inside of the house had as dingy a feel as the outside, like everything was old and hadn't been deep-cleaned in years. Northern custom or not, I didn't take off my shoes. The woman didn't take hers off, either.

She set her bag on the kitchen counter.

I reached for my purse to pull out a notebook. Even though I didn't need to take notes, she might find it suspicious if I didn't. I paused, my hand on my purse. On second thought, I had a better idea. "I'm going to take notes on my phone if you don't mind."

She shrugged. "Suit yourself."

I tapped my screen away from the open call with Vivienne and switched to my Notes app. Having my phone out, with a good excuse for it, would allow Vivienne an even clearer line. The woman didn't seem like she was going to try to hurt me, but I'd been wrong before. And I had my baby to think about now.

I glanced at the little boy who hung around the corner of the living room and kitchen. He had the same unwashed look as the rest of the place.

My heart felt like someone was trying to fit it into a matchbox. Where were this woman's instincts to protect and care for her child? My baby wasn't even born yet, and I wanted to shield him or her from every danger in the world.

As much as I knew I shouldn't judge, I couldn't help it. I could see how it must have triggered Connie. She'd desperately wanted a baby, would have been a great mom by all accounts, and she couldn't have one. But a woman who neglected her child got to have one.

I had to stay focused. I couldn't let my heart sidetrack me. "Just for the record, what's your full name?"

"Theresa Fillmore." She narrowed her eyes at me. "Shouldn't you know that already if you were supposed to talk to me?"

She might not be the best mom, but she wasn't stupid. "I needed to confirm, for the record. I might have gotten the wrong house. Like the first time."

That seemed to appease her. She dropped sulkily into the chair across from me. She didn't offer me anything to eat or drink.

She was going to be suspicious of anything I said. My best chance at getting her to talk might be to make her think I blamed Connie for her own death.

My skin felt tight at the thought.

"What I'm basically trying to do is get an idea of who Mrs. Burke was by talking to her neighbors and other people who might have known her. Usually, when someone is murdered, they did something to bring it about."

The words made me want to gag. Hopefully Vivienne would

know why I was saying what I said. Hopefully she wouldn't think I meant it.

Theresa's head moved subtly up and down. "I could see that. She was nosy. She liked to push herself into other people's business. Thought she knew better than everyone else how to do things."

Like mother their child was the upspoken part of the sentence.

Let's see how far I could get her to take that before I had to pivot to another topic to keep her from getting suspicious. I tapped the words *nosy* and *pushy* into my Notes file to keep up my cover. "Could you give me an example?"

In the quiet that followed, her little boy dragged a chair over to the counter and climbed up on it. He leaned over the grocery store bag and buried one arm deep inside. He came up with a bag of Swedish fish.

Theresa glanced at him and smiled. She turned back to me, and the smile vanished. "She tried to get DJ taken away from me, for example. She tried to tell the social services people I wasn't taking good care of him. She doesn't even have kids, but thinks she knows better."

Her expression said that she expected me to take her side because I was clearly a mom, or about to be one, too. I made an understanding noise.

DJ reached for a steak knife and sawed the package open. My stomach tensed so tightly it felt like a cramp. One slip and he could cut himself. The package gave way. He dropped the knife back on the counter, pushed the chair back to the table, and took off with his treat.

Had he had any real food to eat today, or did she let him have whatever junk he wanted so long as he was quiet?

"My ex was the same way," Theresa said. "Always after me about not drinking when I was watching DJ, but I never drink so much that it's a problem."

How was I supposed to walk out of here and leave that little boy?

But social services had been here. Surely if they'd found anything worse than too much candy and too many cookies, they would have done something, wouldn't they? Unless she hid the evidence of whatever else might be happening. Social services would have had a hard time proving that she'd left him alone since they'd have had to catch her at it. And who knew what else happened behind closed doors?

13

I slid back into the car with Vivienne and turned my phone's volume back to a more normal level.

She tapped the End button on our call and pulled her ear buds out of her ears. "She didn't like Connie."

I nodded. *Didn't like Connie* was an understated way to say it. Every time Connie's name came up in the conversation, Theresa looked like she would have enjoyed spitting on Connie's corpse if she'd had the chance.

As soon as I'd tried to edge the conversation toward whether Theresa had been home the night Connie died, she gotten evasive, saying she didn't see how that helped figure out what kind of a person Connie had been.

My attempt to point out that she might have seen or heard something that could be helpful resulted in a blank stare, followed by, "I don't know anything about it."

"She's hiding something," Vivienne said.

"But what? She could have left her son home alone. She might have been too drunk to properly take care of him."

Or she might have killed Connie. Any of the three options would get her in trouble, either with the police or with child protective services. Any of the three gave her a good reason to lie about that night and refuse to answer any more of my questions.

Normally, I'd put Hal to work digging into Theresa's life to find out her routines and whether we could dig up anything useful. But since Hal and Anderson were both back from their vacations, I knew Anderson had already dropped a lot of work onto Hal's firm. Anderson came home feeling behind. He'd been working ten- to twelve-hour days.

I didn't want to wait a week or two for Hal to climb out from under the load Anderson—and likely his other clients—had dumped on him.

Even though Jay wasn't a trained private investigator, he might be able to at least get me some preliminary information on Theresa while we waited for Hal to have time. When I'd suggested Anderson make more use of Jay since that's why we hired him, he'd said he didn't have time to train someone until he got things under control. Jay wouldn't be as busy as everyone else.

"Ms. Fitzhen...err...Nicole," Jay said before the phone had rung one full time. "I was about to call you. Have I done something wrong?"

Hadn't we cleared this up the last time we talked? "What makes you think you might have done something wrong?" I decided to be gracious and leave off the snarky *this time*. I could be as patient as necessary with someone who was insecure about their abilities, but I didn't want to have to keep telling Jay that he hadn't done anything that would make me fire him.

"Mr. Taylor has me doing tasks that the paralegals and secretary could handle." There was a dejected tone to his voice like he thought he'd come in to work any day now and find an old-fashioned pink slip waiting for him.

Anderson had been more serious than I thought about not wanting to take the time to train Jay at present. Even without training him, he could have given Jay more than what our other employees had already been handling.

And he could have explained to Jay that this was temporary. But Anderson wasn't one to hold an employee's hand any more than my dad was.

"He told me he plans to train you as soon as he gets caught up a little." It sounded worse than I'd thought it would when I said it. It sounded like Jay hadn't gone to law school or like he was too incompetent to remember anything he'd learned. "Anderson has a specific way he likes things done."

"Oh. Okay."

Based on the still-downtrodden tone to Jay's voice, my tacked-on sentence hadn't softened the blow much.

I didn't want Jay to quit on us. He needed self-confidence, yes, but he had good instincts, and that counted for a lot. I had to say something else. "And I wanted to be sure you'd have time to help with my case. I need you to dig into the background of a person I think could have had something to do with Connie Burke's murder. We need to try to find out where she was during time of death and whether she would have had time to plant the blood on our client."

I gave Jay the information, then listened to almost five minutes of him promising he wouldn't let me down. He'd dig up everything that could possibly he useful to our case.

I finally disconnected the call.

Vivienne was smiling at me. "Your volume was turned up loud enough that I overheard. Consider it parenting practice. Children pick the worst possible time to want your reassurance, and they're always looking for your approval, whether they realize it or not."

Vivienne didn't realize it, but she could have been talking about me and my parents. It'd taken me years to realize that I was still seeking their approval, even long after I'd become an adult.

All I could do was try not to make the same mistakes with my baby. I'd learn from the ways my parents had succeeded, and also the ways they'd let me down. Hopefully.

Though, if life had taught me anything, it was that I'd also make a whole lot of brand-new mistakes along the way.

andy, Mark's mom, and I spent the next two days filling our upright freezer with casseroles, soups, and what Mark's mom called *dump-and-go meals* for the crockpot that had previously been collecting dust in the cupboard.

The sight of them working side by side at my counter made my eyes water.

Mandy glanced my way right as I swiped at my face. "Onion?"

"Hormones."

Mark's mom grinned. "When Elise was pregnant, she didn't get weepy. She got the giggles. Grant and Meagan had to forbid her from going anywhere near the funeral home after she came to pick up the boys and something about one of the mourners in line for a visitation set her off."

"Did you ever find out what it was?" Mandy asked.

"Nope. Every time we tried to ask, she broke down laughing so hard she could barely breathe."

I opened my mouth to ask what Meagan had been like while

pregnant, but my cell phone rang. The screen listed my office. I wiped my hands on the apron Mandy had loaned me and swiped my finger across the screen.

"You're not going to believe what I found." Jay's voice reminded me of a puppy jumping up and down in excitement that its people had come home. "About Theresa Fillmore," he added belatedly as if I might not remember the task I'd assigned him.

I motioned to Mandy and Mark's mom that I needed to take the call. Unfortunately, we didn't have an office on the main floor, and my stairs looked longer and higher every day. I also didn't want to go outside. Even though fall was coming, the baby seemed to have turned my thermostat up too high.

I ducked into the laundry room instead. Then silently thanked God that Jay and I weren't on FaceTime. It wouldn't exactly have been professional to talk with my bras hanging to dry in the background and dog hair dust bunnies in every corner. I'd closed the laundry room door before Mandy and Mark's mom showed up on purpose.

I closed it behind me again now to keep the conversation private. "Was she home at the time of Connie Burke's murder?"

Ideally, we wanted to be able to place Theresa Fillmore home or coming home at the time of Connie's death. Even better if we could find someone who'd seen Theresa going over to Connie's that morning. When Jay had texted me last, he'd said he planned to speak with Theresa's boss and then canvas Connie's neighborhood, speaking to everyone from the neighbors to the paper boy and mail lady. Anyone who might have been around very early in the morning could have unexpectedly seen something that would be important only in hindsight. The memory of someone going into a house wouldn't be something people would automatically report since there wasn't anything inherently wrong with it, especially if they lived in the neighborhood.

Jay hadn't said anything while I'd been thinking over what he might have found. "Jay? Were you able to place Theresa at Connie's house?"

"Well…no. She was at work and she didn't get off until well after the time of death window." His voice had a hurried quality to it like he thought I might hang up on him now that he'd failed to find what we needed. "But I remember you saying that you thought Mrs. Burke might have been killed because she wanted to protect Theresa's son. That got me wondering if anyone was staying with a kid that young at night while his mom was at work."

I started to bounce on my toes, only to remember that it'd probably bring on a dizzy spell if I did. "Did you find a babysitter who saw something?"

The police wouldn't have thought to check whether the Fillmores had a babysitter. If the babysitter had seen someone and could positively confirm that person wasn't Nelson, he could be free by the end of the day.

"Not exactly," Jay said. His voice had turned hesitant.

"What does *not exactly* mean?"

"Not at all, actually. But I still think you'll be happy once I tell you."

So this wasn't about our case at all? I slumped against Velma's crate, but I couldn't let on to Jay. He sounded so excited, like he was convinced he'd done something that would make sure he didn't end up fired anytime soon. "You have the floor."

"I went to talk to Ms. Fillmore's boss first." He sounded like he was grinning. "He told me she was working the one to nine shift, so there was no way she could have killed Mrs. Burke. He even checked the convenience store cameras for me, and it showed her there the whole time. But he also confessed that he pays her cash."

Paying cash could mean that neither of them was declaring the income. Not legal, but not all that unusual. Surely Jay wasn't excited simply because he might have caught her cheating on her taxes. Showing that someone committed one crime wasn't enough to have the police look into them for another crime.

I waited.

"That made me suspicious." Jay's voice shifted, taking on a slightly uncertain tone like he could tell I was questioning where he was going with this. "I kept thinking about that kid, and I thought that maybe if she was convicted of something, even tax evasion, it might be enough for child protective services to get involved."

Now it made sense. Jay had either figured out how worried I was over Theresa Fillmore's son, he suspected that more than neglect was going on if Connie had felt she needed to kidnap the child, or he was counting on my pregnancy hormones to give him brownie points if he helped a child. Perhaps a combination of the two.

Still, tax evasion wasn't going to get the little boy into a safer space anytime soon. Though perhaps child protective services could at least mandate parenting classes or something. It'd be better than the situation he was in now.

"Her name popped up when I had a background check run." The hesitancy was gone from Jay's voice. He had that nervous-excited tone of someone anticipating something good. "She's wanted in Colorado for abducting her son during a custody dispute."

Holy crap. No way. "Did you report this?"

He must have forgotten I couldn't see him nod, because there was a bit of a gap. "Theresa Fillmore's been arrested and the little boy is in an emergency foster home until his dad and grandparents can fly in tomorrow morning. From the newspaper clippings that turned up, he sounds like a really nice guy. They've been looking for the little boy for almost a year."

My body felt like all the bones had dissolved. What would have happened had Connie kidnapped that little boy? His dad would have never known what had happened to him and might have spent the rest of his life hunting for his son. Or, perhaps, Connie would have been caught and the little boy would have already been back with his dad.

None of that mattered, though. The little boy was safe, about to be reunited with people who loved him and would hopefully take better care of him.

Unfortunately, we were back at square one again for suspects. Theresa Fillmore couldn't be our murderer.

MARK CAME HOME THAT EVENING WITH BAGS OF TAKE-OUT FROM A Salt & Battery. Technically, I should have had plenty of food waiting for him, but after a full day cooking, I hadn't wanted to use up anything that could be saved for after the baby was born. Besides, I had a craving for fried fish and tartar sauce. Tartar sauce was another olive mystery—I'd hated it before I got pregnant, and now I wanted to slather my entire piece of fish in it.

The real question was whether I'd still like olives and tartar sauce once the baby was out in the world.

Over dinner, I updated Mark on how the person I suspected in

Nelson Burke's case had turned out to have an alibi, but that the story had a happy ending anyway. Thanks to Jay.

The excitement in Jay's voice over what he'd done kept poking at my heart. Anderson had hired him because our firm needed another lawyer, but more and more, Jay felt like someone I could help train. He cared. He cared not only about the case but also about the people we ran into along the way. That level of caring was rare among criminal lawyers. Our firm wasn't likely to have enough innocent clients come in for both of us, but anytime I was working a case, I'd want Jay's assistance.

Mark cleaned up the dishes so that I could stay off my feet. I'd had to do most of my part of the prep work sitting down today.

"Would it cheer you up to look at conference sessions?" Mark asked once everything was cleared away.

Had I not been in the middle of a case and too big to comfortably sit immobile for hours, I would have loved to go with him. While not all the sessions would be applicable to what I did, the more I knew about forensics and other investigative techniques, the better able I'd be to spot holes in a case and areas that should have been investigated more but weren't.

Maybe my mom was right that I wouldn't be able to stop working even once the baby was born. Maybe it was too much of who I was.

I took the seat next to Mark. He'd laid the conference schedule out onto the table with the sessions he was interested in highlighted.

"Are there any you'd prefer I go to?" he asked. "I can take notes to bring home."

I ran my finger down the papers, checking the sessions. Mark switched one session at my request.

On the page for the second day, I jerked my hand to a stop. Mark had highlighted a session titled *Determining the Age of Bloodstains.*

Mark glanced at where my finger had stalled out. "That's one of the sessions I was telling you about. They've developed a technique that's supposed to be able to tell how old a bloodstain is without destroying the sample. They have it up to eighty percent accuracy when testing samples less than two years old. It'll be a game-changer for being able to narrow down a timeline for crimes."

I couldn't peel my gaze away from the page. I'd missed a possibility. I'd assumed that whoever killed Connie Burke collected her blood and then went to Nelson's apartment and poured it over him right away. That had given us a tight timeline that anyone we suspected had to fit within. They needed time to kill Connie, drive to White Cloud, and plant the blood on Nelson without anyone spotting them.

It was one of the reasons why the police were so certain Nelson killed Connie.

But if the blood on Nelson might have been collected from Connie when she was killed but then planted on Nelson hours later, it would change the suspect pool.

Mark was giving me the look that said he knew I'd figured something out, and he was waiting for me to put all the pieces enough into place in my own brain to be able to articulate it to him.

"How sensitive is it?"

"You mean in determining the age of the blood?"

I nodded.

"The last paper I read said that they could tell if a bloodstain was hours versus days versus weeks or months old."

The air seemed trapped in my lungs, like it was afraid if I let it out, I wouldn't be able to draw enough back in again. "I know it's a prototype, but is there any way we can get our hands on one?"

15

_I_ zipped up my hospital bag and set it by the back door. My doctor and Elise had both said I should pack up toiletries, a change of clothes, and a book or two well in advance of when I thought I'd need it. The baby's due date was still a month away, but now seemed as good a time as any.

I'd needed a break from Nelson Burke's case anyway. We were at a standstill with new information until the results came back from the bloodstains.

Mark had called in a lot of favors, but Chief McTavish and the developers of the prototype had agreed to have the bloodstain samples tested. The samples had been overnighted to the lab. Sending them quickly had been the only way to ensure they'd be able to test them before they had to pack everything up for the conference.

My phone rang in my earbuds, automatically switching away from the audiobook I'd been listening to. Mark's picture filled the screen.

"We have the results," he said, rather than making me suffer through a hello and asking how my day had been.

He knew how my day had been. I felt the time slipping away. Even if I went back to work after the baby was born, I wouldn't be going back right away. I needed to get as much in place before I left as possible.

"And?" I asked.

The sound of wind filled the phone as if Mark were walking from his office to his car. He was probably headed out on another call, but had taken the time to call me anyway.

"And there's a significant time gap between the sample from Connie Burke's shirt and Nelson Burke's shirt."

"I don't know whether to be glad or not." The words slipped out before I could stop them.

"It means the priests could have been involved in her death."

I made an affirmative noise. Mark didn't need me to elaborate. He already knew that I was apathetic about proving Nelson innocent if it meant proving a priest guilty.

But I couldn't decide what was the truth or not based on how much I liked it. Truth wasn't relative.

To that end, I needed the details. "How big did the time gap end up being?"

"That's where things get weird. A day."

What in the world... "You said that their results are only eighty percent accurate, though."

"They ran the test three times to be sure. Same results. I talked to the developer himself, and he doesn't think this is a margin-of-error issue. The blood on Nelson's shirt was the older sample. By a day."

My mind couldn't quite parse the words. I had to be sure I

understood correctly. "Does it test only the age of the bloodstains or the age of the blood?"

"This is confidential. They were planning to reveal it for the first time in the session at the conference and in a paper that will come out in a journal next month. They're now testing both. The blood on Nelson's shirt dried a few hours after the blood on Connie's shirt, but the blood itself was a full twenty-four hours or more older."

Mark and I ended the call after he told me he was headed to a death one town over. He expected the call to be an easy one—police had said it looked like natural causes—but if he wasn't home for dinner, I shouldn't worry.

I gave my overnight bag one more check, but if it hadn't been for my checklist, I wouldn't have even registered the items in it.

If the blood on Nelson had been collected from Connie a day before she'd died, then how had the killer collected it? Like everyone else, I'd assumed the killer drained the blood from Connie while killing her. That wasn't possibly anymore. The killer had the blood sitting around for a day before planting it on Nelson, and we knew Connie was alive the day before.

Based on the police reports, the amount of blood on Nelson was significant, but not necessarily enough to prove the person who'd lost it was dead. So the blood could have been collected from Connie the day before. She might have been a bit weak and light-headed afterward, but she definitely would have been alive enough to call for help had someone taken it from her unwillingly and then left her. Besides, why would the killer take the blood but then wait to kill her? It didn't make sense.

The only thing I could think of was to go back and talk to Father Napier and Father Jesse again. They'd had alibis when we assumed the killer had killed Connie, drained blood from her, and then went directly to plant it on Nelson. Now one of them could have killed Connie, gone back to the rectory and on to the staff meeting, then planted the blood on Nelson after.

It'd been almost eleven o'clock when Nelson showed up at my office. That gave a large window of time to be accounted for.

Unfortunately, it also meant that they would have had to leave Connie to die slowly for the age of the blood and her time of death to line up.

A shiver ran over my skin. That level of gruesomeness seemed completely at odds with both of the priests, even if Father Napier continued to hold to his lie. Then again, Ted Bundy had worked for a suicide hotline, and people described him as handsome and kind. Murderers learned quickly how to lie and deceive, or they got caught.

I reached for my car keys. My fingers touched the metal, and I stopped. I still couldn't drive.

I grabbed my phone instead.

Are you working today? I texted to Elise.

No, Erik is. Her message came back almost immediately. *I'm in the ER with Cameron. Fell and sliced his chin. Two stitches.*

I sent a sad-face emoji and praying hands to let her know I'd be praying for him. Poor little guy.

I'd love Mark's and my child whether the baby turned out to be a boy or a girl, but a girl might be easier, based on what I'd seen of Cameron and Grant and Meagan's kids. Then again, if we started with a boy, any future girl would seem like a breeze.

Either way, Elise wasn't going to be available to drive me anywhere today. Neither was Erik, even if I could have convinced him. Based on the meeting I'd had with Stacey and Russ, I knew they were out in the bush all day, checking our pipes and evaluating the health of the trees. Mandy had Noah, which meant she was off the table, too.

Unless I wanted to explain to someone I wasn't close to why I needed to go to a Catholic church in White Cloud immediately, that left me with one option. Vivienne.

She was not going to like this.

THE DRIVE TO WHITE CLOUD FELT LIKE I WAS BEING TAKEN BY A chauffeur rather than a friend. She parked in the church parking lot and walked with me up to the church. The fall sun was hot enough that my hair stuck to my neck, damp with sweat. The heat wasn't anything compared to summer in Virginia, but it was abnormally hot for late summer/early fall in Michigan.

Whoever changed the church sign seemed to think so, too. The message now read *Too hot to keep changing sign. Sin bad. Jesus good. Details inside.*

My gaze dipped to space below it reserved for the date and time of the next blood drive.

Hadn't there been a blood drive just before Connie's death? If Connie had donated, we'd have our answer for *how* her killer got ahold of her blood. Connie wouldn't have even known.

"Vivienne?"

She'd already gone half way up the sidewalk toward the doors. She turned back but didn't say anything. She just stood there, waiting. She had silent anger down to a fine art.

"When did Connie last donate blood?" I asked.

If Vivienne didn't know, I'd have to work on getting a subpoena for the records belonging to the blood bank. They weren't going to hand out donor information to me without it, and that could take too long. I only had a few weeks left before the baby was supposed to be born.

After that, Nelson would be in Anderson's hands. Anderson was a capable lawyer, better than I was in a lot of ways. But he had too many cases to dig after the little details the way I did that might get Nelson set free. Anderson would focus on building a court case, knowing that they'd have months or years to do it. Anderson also wouldn't care about trying to figure out who'd actually committed the crime.

I cared. I cared about all of that.

I definitely couldn't call my mom any time soon. If she picked up my anxiety and excitement over this case, she'd push until I broke about me going back to work. Whether she was right or wrong about it, that should be Mark's and my decision.

Vivienne gave me a look like she thought I might be playing games with her. "Just before she died."

I pointed at the sign. "The day before?"

She walked back toward me, her steps cautious. She pulled her phone out of her purse and tapped the screen. She had to be checking her calendar. She looked up at me. "Why?"

"Change of plans. We need to find out which volunteers worked the church blood drive that day."

16

"I need you to explain this to me a bit more." Vivienne cross her arms over her chest. "I thought you were convinced Father Napier or Father Jesse had something to do with Connie's death now that the window of opportunity changed."

"Whoever killed Connie collected her blood a day before they planted it on Nelson. I think they stole it when she donated blood at the church's blood drive. The murderer could have walked in and found some way to take her blood, but that seems like it would leave a lot up to chance."

Vivienne's arms lowered down. The day was so hot that the momentary compression of her shirt to her skin had left a light sweat line under her bust. "The murder of Connie and framing of Nelson was too well-planned. They wouldn't have wanted to risk missing Connie when she donated. After a person donates, the blood bags are labeled with a number and bar code, not a name."

That was something I hadn't known. I'd never donated blood. The one time I tried, not only was my iron too low, but I'd fainted as soon as the blood started coming out of my arm. Apparently, I'd then proceeded to twitch like I was having some sort of seizure.

Keeping the blood bags anonymous made sense from a confidentiality perspective. The paperwork would allow authorized people to match identities with bags if necessary, but no one else would know who a specific bag came from post-donation unless they'd seen it happen.

Or had access to the paperwork.

Assuming we were right, our murderer had volunteered at the blood drive.

Vivienne had her phone back out. "Let me call Edna. She's the church secretary, and she might have a list of who volunteered that day."

I didn't know whether to be surprised or not that Vivienne not only knew the church secretary's name and number but that she also believed Edna would give her the information simply because she asked. She truly must have been trying to be involved with the church ever since she found out they'd be staying in Fair Haven.

She went through the preliminary small talk, while I tried not to shift on my feet in impatience like a little kid who needed the bathroom. Vivienne had never struck me as someone who liked a lot of small talk.

"So," Vivienne finally said, her fingers twitching on the edge of her phone, "I'm working on something, and I was wondering if you have a copy of the volunteers from the last blood drive."

Now the small talk made sense. She must have been using that time to try to figure out how to phrase her request so that it sounded like she was doing something for the church without actually lying to the secretary. Vivienne probably wouldn't feel much better about that later than I did when I deceived someone, but being able to get what we needed without technically lying made it so people like me could at least tolerate ourselves.

"Sorry, I don't." Edna's voice was loud enough through Vivienne's phone that I could hear it even without Vivienne putting the call on speaker. "The blood bank handled all that because they needed volunteers to fill out their paperwork."

Vivienne thanked her and disconnected. "Now what?"

The look on her face made me feel a bit like I'd asked a hungry person to give up their last bite of food to a person who'd clearly just finished a feast. She might have been able to justify what she'd just done to herself if she'd gotten the information we needed to serve a greater good. The fact that she'd failed seemed to burrow into her soul and make her question the quasi-lie she'd told.

"Now we go to the blood bank," I said. "Without a warrant, they won't tell us if Connie's blood disappeared, but we might be able to convince them to give us a list of the volunteers. You do go to Holy Cross Catholic Church, after all, and you *are* a regular volunteer."

Vivienne ran her fingers over her eyebrows, a nervous tic that I hadn't seen her use before. Maybe she'd never been nervous enough before.

She might be a police officer's wife, but she'd never been involved in an investigation. She'd never been asked to lie by omission to obtain information.

She'd never had to play on my side before.

Clearly, she didn't like it, but her loyalty to the church and the priests must have convinced her because, instead of arguing with me, she pressed the clicker and unlocked her car.

VIVIENNE'S NERVES HAD SHOWN UP AGAIN ON THE DRIVE THERE. She'd never broken the speed limit before in the times I'd driven with her. I couldn't help wondering if she'd pull the *police chief's wife* card if an officer pulled her over. Since we were outside of Fair Haven, I doubted it. Though, knowing Vivienne, she wouldn't have done it even in Fair Haven. She was married to a man who'd worked for years to keep other officers accountable to the law, after all. She wouldn't be likely to see herself as above it.

She pulled into a space in the parking lot and turned off the car but didn't take off her seatbelt. She didn't even remove her other hand from the steering wheel.

This wasn't right of me. She wasn't a lawyer. She didn't have to be involved in every aspect of this case. Asking her to go in with me was basically asking her to use her church to get information for me.

And Chief McTavish definitely wouldn't like it.

I unsnapped my belt. "You don't need to go in with me. It's more than you signed up for."

Her posture didn't change, but she did bring her other hand down to rest on her knee. "Thank you," she said without looking at me.

"No, thank you for driving me here."

She nodded sharply, and I climbed out of the car.

Not everyone was suited for a profession they had the skills for. Vivienne seemed to have some of the skills that would have made her a good investigator in some capacity. But she didn't have the heart for it. Looking people in the face and lying to them, even bending or omitting the truth, seemed to take something from her.

I wouldn't ask it of her again.

The air conditioning inside the blood bank building made goosebumps pop out on my arms.

A twenty-something blonde woman with her hair in a messy up-do sat behind the counter. She looked up and smiled. "Can I help you?"

Her voice had the faintest Southern accent, like she might have been born there or had parents from there but had lived in the north long enough for it to show up more in the cadence than anywhere else.

"I'm—" I started.

The door leading into the back swung open, and Mr. Bird walked out. Out of the door marked Employees Only.

Crap. I couldn't ask for the volunteer list directly as long as he was around. He was already suspicious of me and why I'd been at the church. There was no way he'd let them hand the list over. I needed to stall.

"Ma'am?" the young woman behind the desk said.

"I'm here about blood donation." The words sounded stupid coming out of my mouth, but I couldn't think of a better excuse for why I was at the blood bank.

The young woman gave me a warm-as-melted-butter smile. "I'm sorry. We can't allow pregnant women to donate. You need all that blood for the baby, you know?"

I nodded. I hadn't actually known, but it made a lot of sense. Mr. Bird was still behind me, near a set of chairs. Out of the corner of my eye, I could see him topping up the pamphlet folders with new material. I had to say something else.

"Umm, actually, I meant I'd like to volunteer to help with blood drives." I put a hand on my stomach. "At least until the baby is born."

"Oh." She visibly perked up, and all the regret left her expression. "Of course. Let me get you a form to fill out."

She opened a drawer and slid a paper and clipboard onto the top of the desk.

A shadow moved beside me, and a man's hand took it from her.

"I'll show her where she can fill this out." Mr. Bird said from much too close. He motioned back toward the chairs where he'd been restocking. "Nice to see you again, Ms. Fitzhenry-Dawes."

Not good. There was no reason for him to step in unless he suspected something. I had to say something to throw him off and make this seem normal. Right now, it kind of looked like I might be following him. Or, at least, it could to a mind that had been so suspicious that he thought I'd been trying to record his confession.

"The church puts such a priority on blood donation." I lowered myself into the hard plastic chair. It cut into my back in a way that made me think they'd get more people coming here to donate if the chairs didn't make it so uncomfortable for them to wait. "I wanted to do something to contribute. Is it hard to become a volunteer?"

He handed me the clipboard with the form. A pen also dangled from a string. Pen theft must be a real thing.

"Nothing complicated about it." He stretched the *about* out. I couldn't help feeling like I'd heard a parody of it before where that slight accent was stretched so the word sounded more like *aboot*. "We just need your name and address, emergency contact, and three references. We prefer one personal, one professional, and one that's a doctor, lawyer, or religious official. Once that's done, we'll take a photocopy of your driver's license, and then we'll call you when everything clears."

I started filling in the information. If I didn't, he'd know I was lying.

Instead of leaving, he pulled the other plastic chair up to the tiny table where the informational materials sat.

Great. He was going to actually babysit me the whole time. If he took my form and walked to me to the door, I'd go away with nothing.

Maybe I could at least find out a little more about how easy it would have been for a volunteer to get their hands on the blood.

"They make it almost as hard to volunteer as to get a passport for the first time." I shot him a quick smile, like I was silly and innocent. Unless he'd looked me up online after our earlier run-in, he might not realize I was a criminal defense attorney. Maybe I did family law or property law. Something where I could be intelligent but wouldn't need to be sneaky. Something unthreatening. "What kinds of things will I be doing if I'm approved?"

Mr. Bird shifted in his chair. It took all my willpower to keep filling out my form rather than glance up and try to analyze his face.

"Our volunteers fill a lot of roles." The words came out slowly, as if he wondered why I didn't know this before coming to volunteer. "Some of them help donors fill out the pre-donation questionnaires. Some of them help set up. Some of them hand out juice and cookies afterward."

I flashed him an even brighter smile. *No threat here*, it hopefully said. "I was going to ask before I got this far along, but I didn't have a chance. I won't have to actually handle the blood, will I?"

I didn't have to fake a shudder. By acting like I didn't want anything to do with the actual blood, it should throw him off from what I really wanted to know—what kind of access volunteers had to the blood.

He huffed out what almost sounded like a forced laugh. "We have trained personnel drawing the blood, and blood bank employees package it for transport back here. The only volunteer who handles the blood from Holy Cross is Father Napier."

The pen slipped slightly as I wrote Russ' name for my professional reference. I kept going like it'd been nothing but a natural slip. I had to say something. Something that would make me sound like a real Catholic so he'd keep talking. "He's the one I've gone to most for confession. He helps with the blood regularly? I would have expected him to be squeamish."

Mr. Bird's chair squeaked like he'd moved it a bit closer to the table. "I thought you preferred Father Jesse for confession. You were there last time I went."

I kept writing even though I knew the number I put down for Russ wasn't accurate. I didn't actually want anyone calling Russ. All I could hope was Mr. Bird didn't suspect me because I wasn't looking the number up. Knowing your coworker's number wasn't that unusual.

I was walking on ice here. If Mr. Bird suspected anything, he could stop talking and show me out of the building. But now that I knew Father Napier had access to the donated blood, I needed more information.

Because if I pointed a finger at Father Napier again without something solid to back up my suspicions, Vivienne might not speak to me again.

I had no idea how to ask *was Father Napier ever alone with the blood* without coming straight out and asking that. The best I could do was fill the last two spots of the form in slowly and keep the conversation going until I figured it out.

"That's why I was trying to get a picture of the confessional times." My voice didn't sound entirely normal to me, but it should sound normal enough that Mr. Bird didn't pick up on it. "I wanted to know when I'd be most likely to find Father Napier. Confession is good for the soul, but I'm more comfortable with just one priest knowing everything."

I glanced up at him. He was watching me with a look that said he wasn't sure if I was playing him. Not a good sign.

He straightened the already-straight pamphlets and nodded slowly. "I didn't start going until I got assigned to the blood drives at Holy Cross. But it helps to have someone give me a penance to clear my conscience. Even the scales and all that, so I don't have to carry it around."

Something about the way he said it made me feel the way I did when I accidentally bit down on an ice cube—like a cold shard poking my nerves. The way he said it sounded like confession was a way to do bad things without worrying because you'd be able to wipe it away later. I wasn't a Catholic, but that wasn't how forgiveness worked in my church. You couldn't be a jerk or steal your neighbor's packages off their porch and not worry about it because you'd confess it the next day.

Was he using that to try to ferret out whether I was a real Catholic, or did he really believe that?

Whatever his motive, I didn't have time to let it distract me. I'd finished the whole form, though the last reference was completely faked. I couldn't exactly put down my pastor as a religious reference or Anderson as a lawyer, and I didn't want to risk anyone doing an Internet search for Tom McClanahan's law office if I simply gave a fake number for him the way I had for Russ. The form had basically become more fictionalized as it went, starting out with my real information and then moving down.

I set the clipboard onto the tiny, round table, but I didn't push it toward him. "You never did tell me how Father Napier reacted to having to handle blood."

I made sure my voice sounded gossipy, like I was looking for an interesting tidbit about my priest that I could pass around. With how suspicious he already seemed of me, it might not work, but I had to try.

He shrugged. "I told him what he needed to do, and then let him do it. Since I was the only blood bank employee left, I couldn't babysit him the whole time."

Father Napier had not only worked with the blood. He'd been alone with the blood.

I had to turn this information over to the police.

And Vivienne was never going to speak to me again.

17

"*I* only have ten minutes," Chief McTavish said before he'd even closed the door to his office behind me. "I have to be in Detroit for a retirement party tonight."

He made it sound like I'd barged in on him. Which I'd done multiple times before, showing up unannounced and asking to see him.

This time, though, he'd called me.

Since I'd already been in town, buying a few last-minute baby items with Mark's mom, she'd offered to bring me by the station. I hadn't given her details of the case, but I had told her that I'd provided the police with new information that I was hoping would convince them to continue investigating Connie Burke's murder regardless of their arrest of her husband.

Chief McTavish tugged at the bottom of his uniform jacket as if he were afraid that pausing here for even a minute would wrinkle it. Whoever was retiring must be important to him. From what both he and Vivienne had told me, they'd never stayed anywhere long, so it was likely someone who'd been above him when he was a new recruit.

Only that suspicion kept the imp in me from going off on some tangent for the sole purpose of teasing him with the delay.

"The paperwork is in process," McTavish said. "As of this afternoon, all the charges against Nelson Burke will be dropped."

I felt like he'd snapped a rubber band across the back of my hand to get my attention. My mouth wanted to hang open like a Venus fly trap waiting for its next meal, but that would make McTavish think I was stranger than he already did.

"Just like that?" I said instead.

"Just like that. Based on the new evidence you turned over, the department and DA believe that Nelson Burke was framed by Father Earnest Napier. If we take Burke to court, we'll be wasting taxpayer money, and you'll have an easy way to cast reasonable doubt."

Nelson would go free. We'd won this one without even going to trial—a good thing since my baby felt like it was growing heavier every day. I wasn't going to make it to trial unless I went with a baby strapped to my back. The thought of that would probably have sent my parents into an apoplectic fit at the unprofessionalism.

Still, McTavish's words landed heavily on my chest.

Nelson would go free, but the evidence I'd turned in had swapped a priest for Nelson. A person who called himself a man of God. A man who was supposed to share my faith and beliefs. Beliefs that said murder was wrong.

It was bad enough when I thought he was simply lying to protect Father Jesse. Taking the life of someone else was so much worse.

My brain wanted to spit it out like my mouth would if I'd decided to suck on a lemon. "What was his motive?"

"Connie Burke was having an affair with one of the other priests at the church. The other priest wanted to end it, but Connie wouldn't let him. She threatened him with exposure. Father Napier knew the Catholic church didn't need any more scandals. He felt this was the only way to protect them all."

My head shook without my conscious direction. Maybe this was all a misunderstanding. I wanted Nelson free, but not if another innocent man ended up taking his place. We had to find Connie's *real* killer. "The only other priest at the church is Father Jesse, and I know he wasn't having an affair with Connie. He was helping her with a serious crisis, and so they were spending a lot of time together. But it was innocent. Ask Vivienne."

Chief McTavish moved around his desk and lowered himself into his chair. He didn't even bother to smooth his suit, and the hurried energy that had been hanging around him a moment before faded like fog on a hot day. "I know."

Not what I'd expected him to say.

Silence hung between us as if he'd forgotten for a moment that he was in a rush. All the arguments I could have levied didn't matter if he already agreed with me.

Then he glanced at the clock on the wall behind me and got up again. "Vivienne already made the same argument when I told her. I couldn't let her find out from anyone else." He sighed. "Whether or not the affair was happening doesn't matter. All that matters is whether Father Napier believed they were having an affair that Father Jesse felt trapped in."

I saw where he was going with the argument. People killed over mistakes all the time. A man thought his wife was cheating on him with his best friend, so he killed either one or both of them, only to discover later that his wife had been faithful the whole time. Or someone killed because they thought they would be the one to inherit and they weren't. Or a whole list of causes.

Father Napier didn't have to kill over the truth. He could kill over a mistaken belief just as easily.

And I had no idea what to do with that. Father Napier's actions did point to guilt. I'd even helped show he had opportunity.

All I wanted as to pull my knees up to my chest and cry. Of course, I couldn't. Not only was I not going to cry in front of Chief McTavish, but I couldn't have pulled my knees up anywhere close to my chest right now.

"Did he admit to anything?" I asked.

McTavish shook his head. "Did you expect he would?"

I supposed not.

Yet, if he hadn't confessed once arrested, that opened up a whole new batch of questions.

If Father Napier thought Father Jesse was having an affair with Connie Burke, why not speak to Father Jesse about it? Had he asked, he would have found out that nothing was going on. Surely one priest could tell another priest things that fell under confidence. Priests had to have their own version of confession the same way that counselors went to counseling, didn't they?

You're not his lawyer, Nik, I reminded myself. *Your client is free. You're officially on maternity leave from this point on.*

Or, if my mom got her way, for the next few weeks. Maybe I could do both. My cases weren't frequent, after all. How much time would it really take away from my family to represent a client once in a while? Especially since Jay seemed interested in learning from me. I wouldn't have to shoulder the whole load of my cases myself anymore.

My head felt tired in the too-many-emotional-questions-to-answer kind of way.

McTavish glanced at the clock again. He needed to leave, but he wasn't saying so in the blunt way he would have in the past. That had to be thanks to my friendship with Vivienne. Or the fact that I was so pregnant I'd probably sink like a rock if someone dropped me in the lake. You didn't rush a pregnant woman. It'd be rude.

I did the wiggle-push that getting up from a chair now required.

"Do you have a ride home?" McTavish asked.

I nodded. Mark's mom was parked outside, waiting for me.

I stopped with my hand on the doorknob. He'd said that he told Vivienne about Father Napier's request, but he'd said it in a way that sounded like an officer reporting facts. This had to have hit Vivienne even worse than it had me since it was her spiritual leader and her church. "How did Vivienne take it?"

If McTavish had been anyone else, I would have said the slight movement he gave was a flinch. "She's angry. With me. She thinks I was blinded by my own personal disagreements with Father Napier."

I held back a flinch of my own. I'd assumed that Vivienne attended church alone. I'd clearly been wrong.

And all of this would leave Vivienne unmoored. Her church wouldn't be the same after this. People wouldn't look at her the same. The other congregants would see them as the ones who'd sent their priest to prison, even though he'd made his own choices. She'd already been struggling to fit in.

If she was also angry at her husband, what did that leave her? She'd been dragged around the country for years due to Chief

McTavish's career choices, and now that they'd finally settled somewhere, she might end up as much as outcast in her church as she'd always felt in the town's where they'd lived along the way.

"Was she right?" My words came out more accusatory than I intended. It wasn't Chief McTavish's fault if Father Napier had killed Connie. He'd only done his job by arresting the person he thought the evidence pointed to.

A bit of red flushed his neck. "We had our debates. He thought the church should be the body to discipline members who sinned and that the state shouldn't have that right. It was an untenable fringe belief, and I made sure he knew it."

I bet that went over well. Father Napier's beliefs gave a whole new meaning to *separation of church and state*. I personally sided with Chief McTavish, but it couldn't have been easy to put himself at odds with his priest. I couldn't help but wonder who had started that conversation and how it came up. Had they invited Father Napier over to dinner one night, and he spearheaded the topic when he found out about Chief McTavish's job?

Focus, Nicole. I really was more tired than I thought if I couldn't even stay on topic. Maybe this abrupt end to the case *was* for the best. I could rest until the baby arrived.

I should say something to Chief McTavish before I left. I just didn't know what. I hadn't heard that kind of heat in his voice before. He had too much pride to defend himself directly, but his tone of voice said it all.

He'd spent his whole career until the past few months in Internal Affairs. He'd moved his wife and family all over because he'd believed that even the police needed policing. He'd done it all because of his strong ethics.

He wouldn't wrongfully send anyone to prison over a disagreement, even if it was a disagreement over the proper execution of justice.

I shouldn't have even suggested it by asking. I wasn't the only one whose faith—or at least faith in people who called themselves Christians—had taken a blow today.

18

_V_ivienne sat on my front steps when I got home, her hands tucked between her knees in a posture that screamed of self-protection.

Mark's truck sat in the driveway as well. He'd have no doubt invited Vivienne to wait inside. Even if she hadn't knocked on the door, the dogs would have let him know that someone was there.

But she'd chosen to sit on the steps and wait for me.

How was I supposed to interpret that?

The most likely case seemed to be that she saw me as a friend and Mark as Chief McTavish's friend and colleague.

Then again, it could be simply her natural reserve. Small talk wasn't easy for her. She'd always been the quietest of the four of us when we got together. Facing the news she'd recently received would only make chatting with anyone that much more challenging for her.

Not to mention that she hadn't gone with Chief McTavish to the retirement party. The party might have been restricted to officers, but that seemed unlikely. As county medical examiner, Mark seemed to end up invited to almost every department's events, and most of those included spouses.

What did that say about the depth of her emotions right now if she hadn't attended with Chief McTavish?

I wasn't a marriage counselor. I'd also been married for under a year. Full of marital advice I was not.

Then again, she didn't strike me as the kind of person who'd go to anyone for marital advice.

She had to be here about Father Napier—the last thing I wanted to talk about with anyone, and especially with her. All I wanted was a nap, despite how early in the day it was.

If I brushed her off, though, I'd be an exceptionally bad friend. I should be grateful she was still talking to me after the part I'd played in all this.

I thanked Mark's mom and climbed out of her van. She and Mark's dad had decided that, with Meagan and Grant's kids, Elise's kids, and now our baby, they needed a family-sized vehicle again. At least if I decided to keep working after the baby was born, I'd be able to take advantage of free and willing babysitters.

Not that having someone to babysit had ever seemed like a problem. Mandy had already begged for the privilege, and I had a suspicion that Stacey was planning for a live-at-Sugarwood playmate for Noah.

I stopped at the bottom of the steps.

Vivienne straightened her posture. "Owen told you?"

The phrasing of her question was specific. Not *have you heard?* She must have asked Chief McTavish to tell me personally.

"He did," I said.

"I want you to take Father Napier's case."

With Nelson free, I might be able to represent Father Napier without a conflict of interest. He probably wouldn't want me as his lawyer, however, given that my evidence was what got him arrested in the first place. Chief McTavish must have spared Vivienne that detail.

The role I played in his arrest wasn't even the biggest problem, though. "I only represent the innocent."

She met my gaze, and there was a confidence there that I hadn't expected. She wasn't sitting on my steps, broken and angry and needing a friend. She was sitting on my steps as a crusader on a mission.

And the only thing I could think was *there goes my nap*. "Vivienne..."

"Father Napier is innocent, and he needs a lawyer who will believe him."

I didn't even know where to start. The curtains moved away from one of the windows, and Mark's face appeared, his eyebrows raised in question. I mouthed the words *give me a minute*. If Vivienne had wanted to have this conversation in front of Mark, she'd have been waiting inside.

Mark wouldn't wait forever. As his conference got closer and so did my due date, he'd started wanting to take my blood pressure twice a day and check that I was taking my vitamins and make sure I was eating and drinking enough.

"Did he tell you he was innocent?" I asked.

Vivienne shook her head.

"Then how do you know?"

"He's a good man." Her gaze stayed firm. "He's the one who

started the blood drive, long before I was a part of the church. In the winter, he organizes a sock-and-glove drive to help support local homeless shelters. When he doesn't have to be at the church, he's visiting the sick and elderly. He's been the driving force behind every good program that drew me to Holy Cross when we moved here. He's not a murderer."

That didn't sound like a man who would murder a woman out of fear of causing a scandal for the Catholic church. It sounded like a man who valued all life—the sick, the infirm, the elderly, and those on the outskirts of society.

He did have the fringe belief of thinking the church should be responsible for administering justice among its members, but nothing I'd read in the Bible suggested that lying was an offense punishable by death. Surely Father Napier would have taken his guide from scripture.

"Will you at least speak to him?" Vivienne asked.

I wanted to say no. I opened my mouth to say no. But the word wouldn't come out.

The rest of the town might see Chief McTavish's confident, reserved wife. I saw myself had life turned out only a little differently. When I'd first come to Fair Haven, I'd struggled to fit in and make friends. Thanks to my Uncle Stan's reputation and my relationship with Mark, my time of transition had been swift. I'd found a place to belong.

Vivienne hadn't yet. She'd been trying to make her place at Holy Cross Catholic Church before all this happened. Anything that I could do to make things easier for her, I should do.

"I can't go today. Mark leaves tomorrow morning for a week, and I want to spend the rest of today with him. If you pick me up tomorrow afternoon, we can go then."

~

FATHER NAPIER WAS BEING HELD IN WHITE CLOUD UNTIL HIS BAIL hearing. I'd expected he'd be in Fair Haven since that was where the crime was, but it sounded like the departments had decided it would be a bigger hassle to transport him than to simply leave him there until the court process could start.

Vivienne came with me into the police station even though I'd told her she wouldn't be allowed to be part of the conversation. What Father Napier said to me would be covered by privilege whether we decided my firm would represent him or not. What Vivienne heard wasn't covered the same way.

We stopped in front of the desk. I'd tried to dress professionally, but my wardrobe of maternity clothes hadn't supplied me with many options that would have been approved by my parents. I'd done my best with a pair of stretchy black pants and a flowing white shirt.

The receptionist looked up from her computer. She didn't smile. That was more normal than in Fair Haven, where the desk clerks always greeted me not only with a smile but also by name. And yet it highlighted the fact that we weren't in Fair Haven.

"I'm here to see Father Earnest Napier," I said. "I was told he's being held here."

The woman glanced at my stomach, and she managed to simultaneously give me a pitying look while also curling her lip a little. Did she think my baby belonged to a priest? What was the world coming to when that was the first assumption?

Then again, he was a priest in jail.

She typed something into her computer, as if they had so many occupants in their few cells that she couldn't remember which one

Father Napier was. She shook her head. "I'm sorry. He's not allowed visitors while he's waiting for bail."

"This is Father Napier's lawyer," Vivienne said.

He might not be allowed visitors, but he couldn't be denied access to his legal counsel. That said, Vivienne had rushed in with too much confidence. Father Napier might have chosen not to call a lawyer yet. Or he might have accepted a state-appointed attorney. Or his lawyer might have already—

"Are you sure you have the right person?" The desk clerk's face remained emotionless this time, but the undercurrent of her voice was almost a sneer. "His lawyer left an hour ago."

I didn't let my gaze slid in Vivienne's direction. She should have let me handle this. She wasn't used to being on the opposite side. She was used to being allied with the police. She'd likely expected they'd let us see Father Napier regardless of whether he'd already seen his legal counsel or not.

I could still fix this. I had to. Not only had I given up my afternoon nap to come here, but I wasn't a Fitzhenry-Dawes for nothing. No Fitzhenry or Dawes let someone mock them, however subtly it'd been done.

If someone tries to demean you, my mom once told me. *Call them on it and put them in their place. Few people are willing to violate the social norms of politeness by pointing out such rudeness that it will immediately re-establish authority.*

Here's hoping she was right and that it didn't simply end up getting us kicked out of the station.

I removed the fancy business card case my parents had gifted me, made sure she was watching me, and snapped it open. I flicked a card out and passed it to her pinched between two fingers. "Father Napier wasn't comfortable with the counsel assigned to him by the diocese." I sent up a quick prayer that *dioceses* was actually the right word or that the desk clerk knew less about the Catholic church than I did. Hopefully God knew my heart was in the right place. I didn't intend to insult the Catholic church. "He's considering switching to my firm. You can look us up if you suspect the card is a fake."

My insides felt as squidgy as pudding, but I kept my expression in my best impression of my mom.

"I wouldn't ever suggest that, Ms. Fitzhenry-Dawes." She didn't give the card back, as if she wanted to either do an Internet search for me once I was gone or have evidence if it turned out I was lying. "I'll call for someone to bring Mr. Napier to the interview room."

Her choice to avoid calling him Father Napier made me think I could have told her that he didn't want the lawyer assigned to him by the conventicle or the league, and she wouldn't have known the difference.

Vivienne took a seat to wait for me while a middle-aged officer led me to a room that looked almost identical to Fair Haven's interview room—bare walls, no windows, and a single table with a few chairs around it.

Father Napier already waited for me inside. They'd taken away his robes and left him in the standard-issue jumper given to prisoners. He looked so average that if I hadn't known he was a priest, I wouldn't have guessed. I would have said he was a banker or an insurance agent with a couple of kids, maybe even a grandchild or two.

He glanced up at me and his lips tightened, creating lines at the edges. "You got it right this time."

I sat down across from him so I could see his face. "Got what right?"

"An appropriate location. This is the place where interviews should take place."

Was he teasing me? I'd taken Father Jesse for the jokester, but maybe he wouldn't have been able to survive long in a parish where his senior priest didn't at least appreciate humor. After all, Father Napier had either agreed to or come up with the humorous messages on the sign.

"When they told me another lawyer was here to see me, I didn't expect it to be you," Father Napier said. "Maybe I should have. Have you come to have me absolve you of guilt?"

Wouldn't that be ironic if I'd gone to a confessional to ask questions and came to an interview room for forgiveness? "I'm a friend of Vivienne McTavish. She's a member of your congregation, and she doesn't believe you're any more guilty than Nelson Burke."

"I know Vivienne," he said.

Then he didn't say anything more. His expression said that he'd like to berate me. That he saw me as targeting him for the sole purpose of freeing Nelson.

And yet there was a softness to his face at moments that said he might be also trying to forgive me for whatever role I'd played in this.

Would a guilty man work so hard to forgive? If he were guilty, then this would be the fair consequence. Surely he'd see it that way, despite having a rationalization for what he'd done.

"Vivienne also wants me to help you if you're innocent."

Whatever war was happening inside of him left his face. "You've told me why Vivienne wants you here. You haven't told me why you're here."

He wasn't jumping to his own defense the way I'd expected

considering I'd basically expressed that I had questions about his innocence.

Why *was* I here? On the surface, I'd come because Vivienne asked me. She'd asked me, and I was her friend, and friends stuck by each other.

But there was also this weird heat in my chest that hadn't gone away since Chief McTavish told me they'd arrested Father Napier. Maybe it went back even further than that. Back to when I found evidence that pointed to him. Or back to when Nelson assured me that whoever said he wanted to divorce Connie had been lying.

Back to that moment when it seemed like a man of God hadn't lived up to what he should have done. "You lied about Nelson Burke wanting a divorce."

Father Napier curled his hands back toward himself and lowered them into his lap. "I did. But I fail to see why that would bring you here. Nelson is free, and my lie no longer matters to your client. It only matters to me."

Was I going to do this? Was I going to have it out with a priest? "It matters to everyone. You're a representative. Why lie? Why put the reputation of your church, your faith, in jeopardy?"

Father Napier sucked in his cheeks, making his jowls more pronounced. "I lied because I made an error in judgment." The words came out strained, like he had more practice hearing confessions than making them...which he likely had. "I'd heard the rumors about Father Jesse visiting Connie Burke's home at odd hours. I knew what people were saying. The police started asking questions, and I wanted to protect Father Jesse and the reputation of the church. I was afraid of what he might have done. I told the lie about Connie before I'd thought it through."

Then he was trapped. Once he'd lied to the police, going back to them and saying anything—even that he thought he'd been mistaken—would have made the police suspicious. They'd have wondered why he said it in the first place. They'd have suspected him. Their focus would have immediately turned to the church.

While admitting what he'd done would have been the right thing to do morally, it would have put him in a worse position than had he said nothing. Or even than if he'd told the police about Connie's friendship with Father Jesse.

"I didn't think the police would use my lie as one of their key pieces of evidence against Connie's husband," Father Napier said softly. "I talked to Father Jesse right away, and realized how mistaken I'd been."

Even if he was telling the truth now, though, no one would believe him. I wasn't even sure I could believe him, and I *wanted* him to be innocent.

A tight, heavy heat filled my chest. "People will see you as a fraud or as an example of how Christianity can't be true when people who call themselves Christians do something like this. They'll think that you'd be willing to kill, too. You already lied. In a murder investigation, no less. You look like a man who'd be willing to do anything."

The words tumbled out. It felt good somehow. Like I'd been holding my breath underwater for too long, and now I'd come up and allowed the air to rush back in. I let the words out, but I felt fuller inside than I'd felt since I learned that the case involved priests.

Until they started to come out, I hadn't realized how angry I'd been with him.

Father Napier straightened slightly rather than wilting under my attack the way I'd expected. "Just because I foolishly committed one sin doesn't mean I'd be willing to commit them all. People without faith find it easy to criticize the church and the Christian faith as a whole when one Christian does something wrong. But Christ came to save broken people, not perfect ones."

He was right. If I didn't believe that, then I didn't have anything to believe in at all. If I didn't believe in mistakes and forgiveness, then I'd gutted my faith. People who believed in God were people who wanted to be better, but they weren't always going to get it right. The wrong choices they made didn't make them villains, and it didn't negate the truth of their beliefs. Anyone who read the Bible would see that. The struggle of faith was talked about throughout the New Testament as believers "worked out their salvation."

I could tell him I believed him and walk away. I had an excuse. I was pregnant, after all. I was so pregnant that I was struggling with dizzy spells. Many people would consider that reason enough to go on early maternity leave.

But I wasn't sure yet what to do about my career once the baby was born.

And if Father Napier were telling the truth, I might be the only one to believe him.

"What did the lawyer sent by the church say?"

Father Napier's face tightened. His jowls moved like a dog's might when they were considering growling. "He wants me to confess and take a plea bargain so we can keep this out of the news as much as possible."

On one level, that had to appeal to him. He'd done what he did to try to protect the reputation of the church. On a deeper level, it'd seem like compounding his sin to accept guilt for something he hadn't done. Not only would it be another lie, it would also be helping the true guilty party escape.

If he wanted to defend himself—and by extension our shared faith—I'd help. "I don't know if I can free you. I don't know if I can figure out who did this in time to avoid a trial or to prove you innocent. But I'm willing to try. I just need you to tell me everything that you know."

"You know it all already," Father Napier said. "I don't know how to prove I didn't do something."

I didn't expect him to. That was part of my job in the same way that listening to confessions was part of his job. Swapping wouldn't get the results either of us wanted.

I did need somewhere to start, though, especially given how short we were on time. If my baby came before I figured this out, Father Napier would be handed over to Anderson and Jay. Anderson didn't care whether his clients were innocent or not. I had a feeling that wouldn't go over well with Father Napier. Besides, I was basically working this case for free now that Nelson wasn't under suspicion anymore.

The blood that had gotten Nelson off and Father Napier arrested seemed to be the best place to start. "The case is built on the fact that someone planted the blood on Nelson, and the new timeline suggests they got that blood from the blood drive Connie donated at the day before."

Father Napier rubbed at his neck in a way that suggested his clerical collar made that particular spot itch. Even though he wore a prison uniform now, old habits and phantom pains were hard to escape. "The officers who questioned me said I could have done it because we had both Connie's address and Nelson's address on file. But I was never alone with the blood."

The police wouldn't have found that to be a compelling defense, and neither would a jury. Anyone would say that.

Plus, it brought us back to the *impossible to prove* category. We couldn't prove that he'd never been alone with the blood or hadn't tucked away Connie's blood donation unless we could show that he'd never had so much as five seconds alone to stash the blood and come back for it later.

Everything came back to the window for taking Connie's blood.

19

"How's the case going?" Mark asked the next evening during our scheduled call.

Hearing his voice made me realize how empty the house had been since he'd been gone, and this was only the second night. Last night, I'd barely been able to sleep. I hadn't known until he wasn't there that'd I'd been able to sleep on my side because I'd been wedging myself between Mark and my body pillow.

"That great?" he said.

He must have read into my silence just how slow a start I was off to with my client swap.

"I know more about blood donation than I ever wanted to."

I'd spent my time since meeting with Father Napier researching the handling and transportation of donated blood. Based on everything I'd read, no one could have stolen Connie's blood once it entered the computer system without someone noticing it'd gone missing. Because of all the safeguards surrounding bloodborne diseases, blood was carefully tracked.

Her blood had to have been stolen before everything from the blood drive reached the blood bank and was entered into the system. That gave us a narrow window of time.

Connie's bag of blood was drawn by a nurse who'd worked the blood drive at Holy Cross for the first time that day. Father Jesse remembered her because he'd taken the time to welcome her while she was drawing Connie's blood. The two women hadn't seemed to know each other, but I had Hal's firm looking into her background anyway for a connection.

The nurse had handed Connie's blood off to one of the male blood bank employees, but she couldn't remember which one had been the one to take Connie's blood specifically. Whoever had taken it should have then given it and the related paperwork to Father Napier and another employee who were packaging it for transport and keeping all the paperwork in order.

If Hal's firm turned up nothing on the nurse, we'd have to start checking every male blood bank employee who'd worked that day for a connection with Connie.

"Speaking of blood donation," Mark said, "you're not actually thinking of volunteering, are you?"

I couldn't even remember if I'd told Mark I'd filled out paperwork to volunteer. "Why?"

"A man from the blood bank called me today to check your references. I thought it might be something to do with work, so I ducked out of a session to take the call. I promised to call him back next week when I get home. I wanted to ask you about it first before I went giving out any personal information."

Well, at least my cover was intact. If Mr. Bird was checking my references, it meant he believed I legitimately wanted to volunteer. "You don't have to call back. I was pretending I wanted to volunteer to get information for the case."

"Good, because your weak stomach is a matter of public record."

"Hardy har har," I said, but I couldn't keep the laughter out of my voice. I was one of the last people who should be volunteering around blood. *Pictures* of blood made me queasy.

"How are you feeling?" His voice softened.

Tears pressed the backs of my eyes, which was a completely irrational response. He'd been gone less than forty-eight hours at this point. "Missing you. Other than that, I'm fine. Vivienne McTavish made me beef stroganoff to thank me for helping Father Napier. She made so much I'm sure I can eat it until you get back and still have leftovers."

"My panel was today. I could get a cab to the airport right now and be home before morning."

Part of me wanted to tell him to do it. I'd lived alone for a lot of years. It shouldn't bother me to be alone now. Yet it did. The bed was too big without him. There was no one to rub my aching back or calm me down when I was convinced that every new twinge was the start of labor pains.

But I'd talked him into going. I wasn't going to call him back now for no reason other than that I missed him and my back felt like I was being stabbed with a kitchen knife. "Some of the best sessions are tomorrow. I'm fine, and I'm taking your mom's suggestion and leaving my door unlocked on the off chance that a dizzy spell makes me pass out and I need to call an ambulance."

Mark's mom had once had to search for a hide-a-key rock to get into my house when I'd been poisoned. She'd convinced me that giving emergency personnel easy access was more important than hanging on to my big-city scruples about locking my door every second. The only people whose lives I'd poked into so far in this case didn't want me dead, so I didn't even have to worry about that with leaving my door unlocked.

"My mom's a smart lady."

Other people might have thought it would worry Mark more to tell him that I had planned for a situation like toppling over and needing help. Mark wasn't most people. He was like me in that having a plan in place made him less concerned, even if it meant thinking about dangerous possibilities.

"Besides," I said, "Stacey's coming over tomorrow night, and we're going to have an old-fashioned movie and sleepover night."

Mark laughed. "I wouldn't want to interrupt that, but you know I make a mean bowl of buttered popcorn."

He did. "I love you, and I'll text you when I get up tomorrow."

"Love you too. Same to the baby."

He didn't sound convinced about staying for the rest of the conference, but at least he wasn't arguing about it. I put my phone up to my belly and let Mark tell the baby himself.

I RUBBED MY EYES, SET MY LAPTOP ASIDE, AND STRETCHED OUT MY back. The sharp pain I'd had in my lower back for most of the afternoon didn't budge. I probably should have asked Mark about it when we talked earlier, but it was too late to call him now. It was *much* too late to call Elise and ask her.

My dogs had been asleep in their crates for hours, and I was starting to have to read every paragraph twice, but going up to bed didn't seem like it would help much. Even with the body pillow that was the same size as I was, I wasn't going to be able to sleep in bed with Mark gone. My backache had gotten worse last night without him.

Tonight, I'd try the couch. I wouldn't have the body pillow, but I'd have something solid behind me to prop me up on my side.

I closed my laptop without shutting down the browser window. I'd go back to my research tomorrow.

I glanced back at the stairs. My pajamas and everything were up there, but I didn't want to risk making the pain in my back worse. If it didn't get better by tomorrow, I'd have to go to the doctor. That, combined with my dizzy spells, meant I'd likely end up on bed rest until the baby was born.

Another pain streaked through my back. Definitely worth it to stay downstairs and dressed. If I passed out from a dizzy spell and didn't answer my phone—or couldn't get up afterward to reach the door—I wanted whoever worried about me first to be able to find me easily.

I eased down onto the couch. It wrapped around me like a hug. I'd never been more thankful for a well-broken-in piece of furniture. Everyone said we'd get less sleep once the baby came, but I couldn't imagine it. I wasn't sleeping much now. At least once the baby was here, I'd sleep soundly and comfortably for the few hours I got.

The pain came again. I wriggled around. Mark's mom had said that changing positions usually made Braxton Hicks contractions stop, but nothing seemed to be helping these ones. I hoped all the female Cavanaughs were wrong about first baby's coming late. Right now, I'd be happy if the baby came as soon as Mark got home rather than waiting out the final couple of weeks. I just wanted my body back so I could reach my toes, sleep on my back, and be able to walk around without dizzy spells.

My eyes drifted shut.

They popped open again. My head felt stuffed full of feathers. I must have been asleep for long enough that my body had tried to cycle down into REM sleep.

My first thought was that either my bladder or another round of Braxton Hicks woke me, but I didn't feel an urgent need for the restroom or cramps in my abdomen. My head started to clear. I should still be asleep. But I wasn't.

The snick of the front door opening carried across the room.

That's what I'd heard. I'd heard someone at the door.

Mark had come home early after all. Maybe I should be annoyed at him, but the truth was that I'd wanted him here. He must have heard it in my voice. And he wanted to be home with me, waiting. It wasn't about fear for him anymore. It was about us preferring to be together. Next time he went to a conference, maybe we could leave our child or children with his parents and make the conference a couple's getaway.

The door eased shut again with an almost inaudible click. He moved across the room and toward the stairs more softly than I'd ever heard him walk. He must be trying not to wake the dogs.

When I first brought Toby home, he'd demanded to sleep in the bedroom with me because that's where he'd slept with his previous owner. I'd worked with him until he would sleep in the laundry room with Velma in their crates now, but if he woke up after he went to sleep, he'd cry the whole night unless we let him up to the bedroom. And with Mark having been away, Velma wouldn't want to go back to sleep either if she figured out he was home.

They'd hear us even if we whispered a welcome.

I wouldn't reveal myself down here. If I surprised him, Mark would likely make a noise and wake the dogs. I'd wait until he made it up the stairs and then I'd follow. He probably wouldn't realize that the body pillow under the blankets wasn't me right away, so he wouldn't be worried as long as I creeped up right after him.

The wood on the stairs creaked. He'd reached the third from the top. It didn't matter where you stepped on that stair. Mark must be tired if he hadn't stepped over it. We usually tried to skip that stair once the dogs were in bed.

I eased up from the couch. Pain arched through my stomach worse than any cramps before. I leaned over and sucked in a deep breath. Stupid Braxton Hicks. These had to be worse than labor— not in intensity, but in duration.

The pain eased, and I straightened up. I picked my way across the floor toward the stairs.

A staccato pop broke the silence from the direction of the bedroom.

Sweat slicked on my forehead, and my hands felt like I'd shoved them into a bucket of snow. A half-asleep woof-growl came from the laundry room.

That was the sound of a silenced gunshot.

Whoever was up there had stepped on the noisy stair.

Whoever was up there wasn't Mark.

I should have known. Mark would have at least texted me when he was on his way home so as not to frighten me by coming into the house at night. He'd never have risked me waking up to see a shadowy figure in our bedroom.

Whoever was up there wanted to kill me.

The man upstairs had shot my body pillow, thinking it was me, asleep in the bed. He'd have known as soon as the pillow's stuffing poofed out the hole rather than blood that it wasn't me.

His footsteps had already gone to the second bedroom. Definitely a man. The tread was wrong for a woman. Too heavy. The strides too long even as he attempted to be quiet.

Then the creak of the hinges that needed replacing on the upstairs bathroom door.

He'd know now that I had to be downstairs. He'd come looking for me.

My body felt encased in plaster. This case hadn't seemed dangerous like the rest. I'd been careful because of the baby. I hadn't gotten onto the radar of whoever the real killer was.

Except I must have. When I'd gone to the blood drive and started asking questions.

Focus, a calm voice in my head that sounded like my mom said. *You have to move. Now.*

My panicked brain snapped back into reality. Now wasn't the time to let my mind spiral out of focus on things that weren't important. The footsteps were moving back toward the stairs.

He'd be at the top of the steps before I could reach the door. I couldn't outrun him, not with a belly full of baby.

I also couldn't go back to the couch. If he'd checked the other rooms, he'd check there, too, assuming I'd have to be sleeping there since I wasn't upstairs.

The only door close enough was the laundry room with the dogs. Velma's barks had already risen to a level that said she knew the person in her house wasn't one who should be there. Toby was barking alongside her, but his voice sounded more tentative and confused.

Hopefully the man wouldn't think to check in the laundry room in the middle of the night. No one would sleep there, and he couldn't know whether the dogs were crated or not.

I tiptoed forward and opened the door as softly as I could. The third-from-the-top step squeaked again.

If I closed the door now, the sound and movement would draw his attention. Would he remember that the door had been closed when he went upstairs?

What was I going to do if he checked this room?

I huddled back by the clothes hamper wedged in next to Velma's crate. Why hadn't I grabbed my phone? I couldn't even call for help. Then again, when I'd left the couch, I'd planned to go upstairs and meet my husband, not a crazy person who'd already killed.

There wasn't even anything here a could leave a note with if I figured out who this was.

I had to figure out who this was before they found me. If I knew that, I might be able to come up with something I could say that would convince them not to kill me. Me and my baby.

My baby. This was supposed to be a safe case. I'd been so careful.

I shouldn't have taken this case. The puzzle wasn't worth it if it put my baby in danger. Nothing was worth putting my baby in danger.

And Mark's mom was never going to forgive herself if I died this way. She'd been the one to convince me to leave the door unlocked because Mark wasn't home.

Would this man have shot Mark, too? That seemed like a huge risk to try to shoot us both before one of us woke up. We might have had a gun ourselves. One of us might have been able to get away long enough to call for her.

Pain pulsed behind my temples to match the next Braxton Hicks.

Unless he knew Mark wasn't going to be home because he'd

called him and Mark had told him he was away. I hadn't put Mark down as a reference on my volunteer form. I'd put him down as my emergency contact.

No one from the blood bank should have called Mark.

I'd written Nicole Cavanaugh on my volunteer paperwork out of habit because it was official paperwork. I'd changed my name after Mark and I got married. I only practiced law under my maiden name.

The only person at the blood bank who could have connected Nicole Cavanaugh with the lawyer Nicole Fitzhenry-Dawes who was poking around into Connie Burke's murder was Mr. Bird.

20

*V*elma's growling bark was so loud I couldn't hear where Mr. Bird's footsteps were anymore. He could have decided I wasn't home and left, or he could be checking the office at the back of the house, which would have given me a chance to escape. Or he could be about to open the laundry room door.

Mr. Bird must have assumed I was getting too close to putting all the pieces together. He'd been smart enough to plan Connie's murder. He must have seen through my questions when I filled in the volunteer paperwork.

He'd already been paranoid about me when he'd caught me near the confessional. I hadn't suspected him at all then, but a guilty conscience would have easily convinced him that I did, especially when I came to the blood bank where he worked. He wouldn't have realized I didn't know he worked there until that moment.

This had to be about his wife's death. Hadn't Father Jesse said something about Bird feeling guilty? And Bird had sounded like he used confession as a way of dealing with things he'd done wrong.

But how did Connie fit in?

His face as he'd found me standing outside the confessional door and how paranoid he'd been about it flashed through my mind. He'd thought the sanctity of the confessional only applied to Father Jesse. If he thought Connie overheard him confessing his wife's murder while she cleaned around the confessional, he wouldn't have known she couldn't go to the police.

A man who'd killed twice wouldn't be talked out of killing me. Not once I'd seen him. What I'd guessed or had evidence to back up wouldn't matter.

Unless I got out of here, my baby and I were going to die.

Velma strained against the front of her crate. She'd drawn her jowls back into a full growl, her long, sharp teeth showing even in the moonlight. He had to be coming closer. I couldn't hear him, but she could.

I'd never seen her that way before. If I didn't know that she wouldn't hurt me, if I didn't know that she was acting this way out of a desire to protect me, I'd have been afraid of her.

Let her protect you, a quiet voice in the back of my head whispered. It didn't sound exactly like my parents or Mark's mom or any of the advice givers I normally heard. It was more like all of them together.

Velma saw her purpose in life since I'd gotten pregnant as protecting me and the baby. She'd been so serious about it that she'd turned against Mark at first.

But if I let her out of her crate, Bird might shoot her.

If I didn't let her out, he would definitely shoot me and kill my baby in the process.

Velma was my only hope of getting out of here alive. Maybe God had given her those protective instincts for this very moment.

I didn't have time to second-guess my decision.

I unlatched her crate door. She launched out of her crate and through the laundry room door.

A shot rang out, followed by a yelp of pain.

What had I done? Had he killed her?

Then a crash, and a man's feral scream rent the air.

21

*P*ain clamped down on my stomach again. A panicked part of my brain tried to tell me that these weren't Braxton Hicks. This time, they were the real thing. Shocks could bring on premature labor.

But I couldn't be in labor right now. Not now.

Snarling and a man's cursing clambered in from the living room. I clutched the edge of Velma's crate and tried to breathe through the pain. I needed to move or I was going to miss my chance.

I stumbled forward. Velma had knocked the door open.

Bird lay on his back a few feet away, Velma on top of him. They were thrashing around too much for me to see clearly what was happening, but it looked like she had latched on to his arm or shoulder and he pummeled her with his free hand.

She had teeth, but he had over a hundred pounds on her. Eventually he'd get free and shoot her. I had to find his gun and get my phone. I couldn't leave my brave girl to that fate. Her fur already looked dark and wet on one side. Besides, if I tried to run and he got free, he'd catch me. I couldn't move fast enough.

I waddled toward the couch and grabbed my phone.

"Fair Haven Police Department," Shelley, one of the people who worked Fair Haven PD's front desk, said.

I'd meant to dial 911, but my fingers must have moved on their own. Pain rippled through my stomach like I had electrodes hooked up to my muscles. This was so much worse than any Braxton Hicks I'd had.

"Send help." My words came out in a gasp. "Police. Ambulance. Vet."

"Nicole?" Shelley's voice had a weird strangled quality to it. I must have sounded worse than I realized. "Nicole, what's going on?"

"A man named Bird"—I didn't even know his first name but Vivienne or Father Jesse would—"broke into my house, trying to shoot me. I have to find the gun."

Shelley sucked in a breath. I could hear her talking to someone but I couldn't catch it all. "Erik and Quincey are on their way. Leave the gun. You need to get out of the house."

"I can't. My dog. Send a veterinarian too, okay?"

On some level, I knew my words were scattered and choked. I wanted to cry. But I needed to find that gun. It wasn't in either of his hands. Bird must have dropped it when Velma tackled him.

If I could just find it, maybe I could make him stop hitting her. I couldn't let him keep hitting her. What kind of damage was he doing?

"I'm staying with you until they get there," Shelley said. "Can you tell me what's happening? Can you get somewhere safe?"

I didn't see the gun anywhere. Velma was losing her grip. She looked tired.

This was about angles. If he'd been coming to the laundry room and she came out of it, he would have fallen back toward the couches. But his arm could have gone sideways, more toward the end table.

I crouched as well as I could. Was that dark lump the gun or a dog toy? Shelley was still talking in my ear.

My breath, my whole body, was unsteady from the last round of pain. I'd tumble over if I tried to reach down. I used the arm of the couch to lower myself to the ground.

The gun lay right in front of me. I'd need both hands to hold it steady. I tapped the speakerphone button and laid my phone on the floor.

I crawled a bit to the side so Bird would be able to see me and leveled the gun at him. "Stop moving or I'll shoot you."

I wasn't sure if I actually would. Or could without hitting Velma. But he didn't know that.

The string of curse words he leveled at me would have made even my reserved father deck him. "Call off your dog."

"Stop moving first. And shut up."

Bird finally did what I told him. Shelley's frantic voice was coming through the phone, telling me the cruiser would be there any second.

I called Velma. She didn't move. I'd trained her to come as soon as I called, but it'd always been a struggle when her attention was elsewhere.

I called her again, and she slowly let go of Bird. I kept the gun trained on him in case he tried to hit her. She backed towards me, keeping her eyes on him, her teeth bared and a growl rolling from her throat. Blood covered her side, and her breathing came heavy. She could barely put weight on her right front leg.

But she was alive. I prayed that our veterinarian could keep her that way.

"He shot Velma," I said to Shelley, raising my voice to be sure she could hear me. She and I had been in dog obedience classes together. She'd know who Velma was. "I need you to send someone to take her to a vet. And an ambulance for him." A warm trickle dribbled over my thighs. Crap. "Make that two ambulances. I'm in labor."

22

*E*rik and Quincey Dornbush burst through my door less than a minute later, guns drawn. Quincey handcuffed Bird and took him out to the car to wait for the ambulance.

I'd squiggled to lean my back against the couch. Velma laid at my feet. She refused to let Erik get anywhere near me. The fact that she was laying down now instead of standing didn't bode well. Unfortunately, her pain seemed to have made her completely unreasonable. All she knew was that she hurt, and she needed to protect me.

"Who would she trust?" Erik kept far enough away so that Velma stopped growling. "Shelley got ahold of your vet, and he'll be waiting at the clinic with a technician for surgery, but you can't take her there."

I wanted to snap at him that I knew that. I'd known before he did that this baby was coming. I wasn't going anywhere other than the hospital no matter how much I wanted to stay with her. She would have trusted Mark, but he was too far away. I'd call him once I was in the ambulance.

There was only one other person who spent enough time with her that she might let them handle her. "Mandy," I gasped out as another contraction hit. Since Mandy wasn't a man, Velma might automatically see her as less of a threat, too.

I tossed Erik my cell phone. The throw went wide but he managed to catch it anyway. Mandy's number was easy to find in my contacts.

He turned his back while he talked to her. Outside, another siren pulled up. Hopefully the ambulance. I didn't know how long labor took, but the pain was so close and hard that I couldn't fully catch my breath in between.

Erik turned back around. "She was at Russ'. She'll be here with her van in less than two minutes."

Erik's phone rang, and he answered, moving away slightly.

Mandy came through the door at the same time as he finished his conversation. She wore a pink robe. I'd never been more grateful that Mandy took everything seriously. She hadn't stopped to dress.

"Russ has the van running." She grabbed Velma's leash off the hook by the door. "You want to go for a walk, puppy girl? Let Auntie Mandy take you for a walk."

Mandy glanced at me and at Velma's side. Her face went gray.

But Velma's tail wagged softly, hitting my foot.

Mandy slowly clicked the leash onto her collar. A diamond ring that hadn't been there before glittered on her ring finger. It seemed like congratulations were in order. But later. When the baby wasn't trying to rip me in two in order to come out.

Mandy made the come-on kissing noise. Velma lurched to her feet and let out a whimper. Mandy slowly coaxed her to the door. She shot me a thumbs up and mimed calling me, then disappeared.

My whole body felt sweaty. "Are the ambulances here?"

Erik knelt on the floor beside me and cleared his throat.

No. No no no. Erik clearing his throat meant something bad was coming.

"The second ambulance is broken down. They're sending another one from White Cloud."

I wrapped a hand around my stomach. We were in trouble. Looking back, none of the contractions I'd been having earlier were Braxton Hicks. I'd probably been in actual labor for over twelve hours based on when the first contractions started. Once Quincey had handcuffed Bird, I'd started timing my contractions as best I could. They weren't as close together as they'd seemed to be when Bird was fighting Velma, but I didn't think that was a good thing. Not when combined with how I felt like I needed to push.

"I don't think I can wait for it to get here." I explained to Erik what was happening. "Why didn't they take me in the first one?" Surely they'd known I was in labor.

Erik cleared his throat again. "Labor takes hours. They thought they had time, and they were afraid Velma might have hit an artery when she bit him." He rose to his feet. "We can take you in the cruiser. Quincey went in the ambulance."

The cruiser. Yes. We didn't need the paramedics. We could get to the hospital. I tried to get to my feet, but another contraction hit strongly enough that my legs gave out. I cried out and slid back to the floor.

"Nikki," Erik's voice was soft, "if we can't make it to the hospital, we're going to have to deliver the baby here. I know what to do... I've just never had to do it before."

Police officers received training in all sorts of emergency situations. But I was not going to have my cousin-in-law looking at my naked lady parts. If only Mark were here. I should have never told him to go. I should have never told him to stay for the remaining days of the conference.

On a distant level, I knew that was the pain talking. We had no way of knowing this would happen. First babies were supposed to go late.

There had to be some other solution. I'd never be able to face Erik again if he delivered my baby. "Call Elise. Elise can come."

Elise had once shot a man in the head for me and then pulled me out from under his dead body. It wouldn't be so bad if it was Elise.

"I can try, but she might not make it in time based on what you've told me. I at least need to check you."

"Call her first." I knew I was being irrational, but I couldn't seem to help it. It wasn't supposed to happen this way. I was supposed to have Mark with me. I wasn't supposed to have a baby on my living room floor with only Erik for company. "Call Elise."

A woman's form jogged through the door. "I'm here." Elise came into focus despite my bleary eyes. "I got in the car as soon as I heard your address and the code on the scanner. What's happening?"

I wanted to ask why she was sleeping with the police scanner on, but I didn't really need to. She'd have been sleeping with it on when Erik was on night shift because she'd want to know if he got called into anything dangerous. Elise was nearly as paranoid as I was.

Erik filled her in.

She motioned at Erik and then toward the door. "The kids are in the car. I couldn't leave them alone, and I didn't want to wait for someone to come. I need you to call Stacey to take them. She's closest. Then help me gather towels and stuff."

Tears sprang into my eyes, and this time I didn't stop them. I'd never loved the family we'd built in Fair Haven more than I did now.

23

Mark sat on the side of my hospital bed and pulled back the edge of the baby blanket to stroke our daughter's cheek. It turned out I hadn't been that far off believing he'd been the one who came into the house in the middle of the night. Despite me recommending he stay at the conference, he'd hopped a plane anyway. Our daughter and I arrived at the hospital at the same time as he did.

If our baby had been a boy, we'd planned to name him Stan after my uncle. That way no one could have felt left out, and it was a family name, which would have made my mom happy.

A girl was more challenging. We hadn't been able to come up with a name before she was born, and we'd thought we'd still have a few weeks.

We'd talked about naming her Elise, now that Elise helped bring her safely into the world. Elise had objected that'd be too confusing, but said she'd take the honor of having it as the baby's middle name.

In the end, we went with Emma Elise Cavanaugh. Emma had been the name Mark's mom picked out for a girl and never got to use after giving birth to four boys. It seemed like a way to have a "family" name without adding confusing repetition.

Mark leaned in and gave me a kiss. "Why don't I take her so you can get some rest?"

I needed it. I'd been exhausted all day, but we'd had an almost steady stream of visitors. Mandy and Russ had been the last. Mandy had insisted that they stay with Velma until she woke up from the anesthetic and the vet checked her. The bullet had come out easily, and he was confident she'd make a full recovery.

As tired as I was, though, I wasn't going to be able to rest easy until I knew what was happening with Mr. Bird. "Can you call Chief McTavish first?"

Vivienne had already been by, and she told us that Damon Bird had asked for a lawyer and wanted to confess in exchange for something less than life without parole. After two murders and an attempted third, that's what he'd be facing otherwise.

Mark dialed and put the phone on speaker.

"I wondered how long you'd be able to stay away from the case," McTavish said. "Even being a mom isn't enough to keep you out of it."

He wasn't right about that, but now wasn't the time to tell him. I'd already told Mark. I wasn't going back to work until any children we had were older.

Part of it was that I wanted to spend as much time with Emma and any others who came along as possible. I didn't want to be the kind of mom who wasn't there when they needed me because I was working.

But it was also more than that. Damon Bird broke into my house. He almost killed Emma along with me. Had she been two or four or six and someone broke into our house, what would have happened? I couldn't take that risk. While my kids were little, I had to put protecting them first. I'd still consult a little when Anderson needed me, and I'd still train Jay, but I was done with taking cases for the foreseeable future.

Strangely, I was okay with that.

"Turns out," McTavish continued, "that he's Canadian. He married his wife to get into the country. The plan was always to get a divorce after he'd had time to become a citizen on his own. Except I guess she decided she didn't want that unless he paid her a very large amount of alimony. He decided it'd be easier to kill her instead."

His Canadian heritage explained the slight accent I'd had trouble placing.

"What about Connie?" I asked.

"Your guess was pretty accurate. She was outside the confessional cleaning one day when he came out. He thought she might have overheard him confessing to killing his wife. He started to follow her, and heard her ask Father Jesse what she should do if she knew someone had done something wrong."

That had to be the first time she'd brought up her neighbor to Father Jesse. Damon Bird wouldn't have known that, though. He'd have assumed she was asking about what she'd overheard while he was in the confessional.

A sound filled McTavish's end like he was flipping the page in a notebook to make sure he got the details right. "He already had her address and Nelson's address from her volunteer form for working the blood drive. All it took after that was striking up a few conversations with her to find out the things he needed to know, like that she lived alone and Nelson was out of town most of the time as a pilot."

With her home address, he could have also easily watched for patterns in her neighborhood. He'd picked a time when both neighbors would be done, giving him added privacy.

"Why take the risk of pouring the blood on Nelson?" Mark asked. "He might have gotten away with it if he didn't do that."

He might have. Had we not checked the age of the blood, we wouldn't have known it had to have been stolen the day before at the blood drive.

"He planned to pour it on Nelson's carpet while Nelson was out of town. He didn't expect him to be home. Once he was, he thought it'd be even better. There was this case back when he lived in Toronto. Some guy drove his car to murder his in-laws, all while asleep. Bird figured Nelson's lawyer would argue the same type of thing and the case would be over quickly."

I groaned. Mark raised his eyebrows in question.

"Mandy can't ever find out. She told me about that news story. If she finds out she was even remotely right, you'll have bigger troubles than me meddling in your cases, Chief."

Mark chuckled. "Russ will probably keep her out of too much trouble."

Maybe he would.

I looked down into Emma's sleeping face. So many unexpected blessings had come from my Uncle Stan leaving me a maple syrup farm.

And once whatever children God blessed us with were old enough that I felt safe practicing again, my job would still be waiting for me.

In the meantime, I'd found something that I loved even more.

LETTER FROM THE AUTHOR

When I first started this series, I didn't realize I would find so many stories to tell about Nicole, Mark, and their friends. In fact, I thought I was done after book 9, but here we are at book 13!

This will be the final Maple Syrup Mysteries for a little while at least. It's time for me to turn my attention to Isabel Addington and the Cupcake Truck Mysteries. If you've enjoyed the Maple Syrup Mysteries, I hope you'll join me for this new series.

Book 1 (*Sugar and Vice*) is already available, with more books in the series scheduled for release in 2020.

And I'm already brainstorming the series that will follow. If you love animals, you'll love what I'm planning!

Please sign up for my newsletter. I announce new releases there first. I share recipes and other exclusives. I also give my newsletter subscribers a free ebook copy of *Sapped*, a Maple Syrup Mysteries prequel.

You can sign up at www.smarturl.it/emilyjames.

Love,

Emily

ABOUT THE AUTHOR

Emily James grew up watching TV shows like *Matlock*, *Monk*, and *Murder She Wrote*. (It's pure coincidence that they all begin with an M.) It was no surprise to anyone when she turned into a mystery writer.

Alongside being a writer, she's also a wife, an animal lover, and a new artist. She likes coffee and painting and drinking coffee while painting. She also enjoys cooking. She tries not to do that while painting because, well, you shouldn't eat paint.

Emily and her husband share their home with a blue Great Dane, a Boxer-mix, seven cats (all rescues), and a budgie (who is both the littlest and the loudest).

If you'd like to know as soon as Emily's next mystery releases, please join her newsletter list at www.smarturl.it/emilyjames.